Strength of a Vampire
Seattle Vampire Tales Book Two

I stand on the landing, forehead pressed to the door. On the far side, Maggie's breath comes in ragged gasps. "Dammit, Rix," she growls, thumping the door. I've never known her to be so angry, and feel awful for being the cause. Can she ever move past this? Her stomping feet fade away. Turning, I descend the stairs.

...

Ten minutes later, I'm outside, staring at a key too heavy to lift. I somehow manage to lock the door. Swallowing tears, I cross the backyard to the little fountain. Its burbling in the moss-covered hush calms me. I slip the reluctant key into the basin. It creeps slowly down, clinging to the rough granite, until it disappears beneath the ripples of the tiny cascade.

Praise for
Strength of a Vampire

Ridgewell's story of a Seattle-based vampire sub-culture during Covid and the George Floyd demonstrations provides an unforgettable mix of vampire and human characters who interact in the parks, alleys, and on the freeways of her nighttime city to produce an unforgettable romance, suspense, and horror novel.

— SEELYE MARTIN

Rix is trying survive in a Seattle locked down for Covid. And he's in love with a human woman, Maggie, an ER nurse always in danger from this new disease, while Rix himself also worries about vampire hunters that are killing his kind.

This is a deeply compassionate novel about a vampire who wants to do the right thing by everyone — human and vampire — in a hostile and difficult world. It's a beautiful and compelling read, and an accurate account of the years Covid hit Seattle.

— KEYAN BOWES

BOOK COVER DESCRIPTION

In the peachy light of dawn, the backs of two people are shown watching the abduction of a third by men in black riot gear. Medium-sized stylized white text in the upper right reads, "SEATTLE VAMPIRE TALES" with "BOOK TWO" just below it in a much smaller font. At the bottom, in much larger text it reads, "STRENGTH OF A VAMPIRE" with "RAMONA RIDGEWELL" just below it in small font.

ALSO BY RAMONA RIDGEWELL

Seattle Vampire Tales

Being a Vampire (Book One)

Strength of a Vampire (Book Two)

Blood of a Vampire (Book Three) *

* Forthcoming from Intrepid Turtle Press

Other

Two Hour Transport 2 (co-editor/contributor)

Eccentric Orbits: An Anthology of Sci-Fi Poetry Volume 4

Eccentric Orbits: An Anthology of Sci-Fi Poetry Volume 5

STRENGTH OF A VAMPIRE

SEATTLE VAMPIRE TALES
BOOK 2

RAMONA RIDGEWELL

Intrepid
Turtle Press

Strength of a Vampire
Seattle Vampire Tales Book Two

This is book is entirely a work of fiction. Names, characters, places
and incidents are the products of the author's imagination or are
used fictitiously, though reference may be made to actual historical
events or existing locations.

First edition: January 2025
Intrepid Turtle Press
2442 Market St NW #393
Seattle, WA 98107

Cover illustration and design by Jamie Noble Frier (The Noble Artist)

Print ISBN-13: 979-8-9908723-2-5
eBook ISBN-13: 979-8-9908723-3-2
Library of Congress Control Number: 2024917891

NOTES TO READERS

Thanks so much for taking an interest in my story. It's filled with vampires eking out an existence in modern-day Seattle, and picks up where "Being a Vampire" left off, with the COVID-19 pandemic and the early-summer protests in Seattle raging. The main character, a vampire named Rix, relates what he is observing—an impartial witness to a defining moment in history. But no one is immune from the impacts of the upheaval of 2020.

This content is not intended for children or youth due to violence, sexual situations and other adult themes.

Because of potentially triggering circumstances, I included content warnings at the scene level in the Footnotes at the end of the book. The Footnotes also include links to real places and events that happen in the story.

Key content warnings and triggers include:
- vampire violence (of course)
- allusions to past child sexual abuse/rape
- the COVID pandemic

- food, housing and employment insecurities

- George Floyd/BLM protests, including violence against protesters

- deaths, including: one human teen who dies of COVID; a murder/attempted suicide by one of the vampires against another vampire; several other vampire deaths

- abductions of vampires

RAINN is the National Sexual Assault Hotline: Confidential 24/7 Support. https://www.rainn.org/resources.

988 Suicide & Crisis Lifeline is a national organization that provides 24/7, free and confidential support for people in distress, among other services. https://988life line.org/ or call 988.

I wrote this story as the real-world events were unfolding, so many of the reactions, comments and incredulity were my own, just told via my characters. An example of a pair of scenes written in the moment are the adjacent scenes in Volume 3, Vampire House, the final one in Chapter 3: Protesting, and the first one in Chapter 4: Tenuous Tendrils, which document the first night of the George Floyd protests in Seattle.

I hope you enjoy the story.

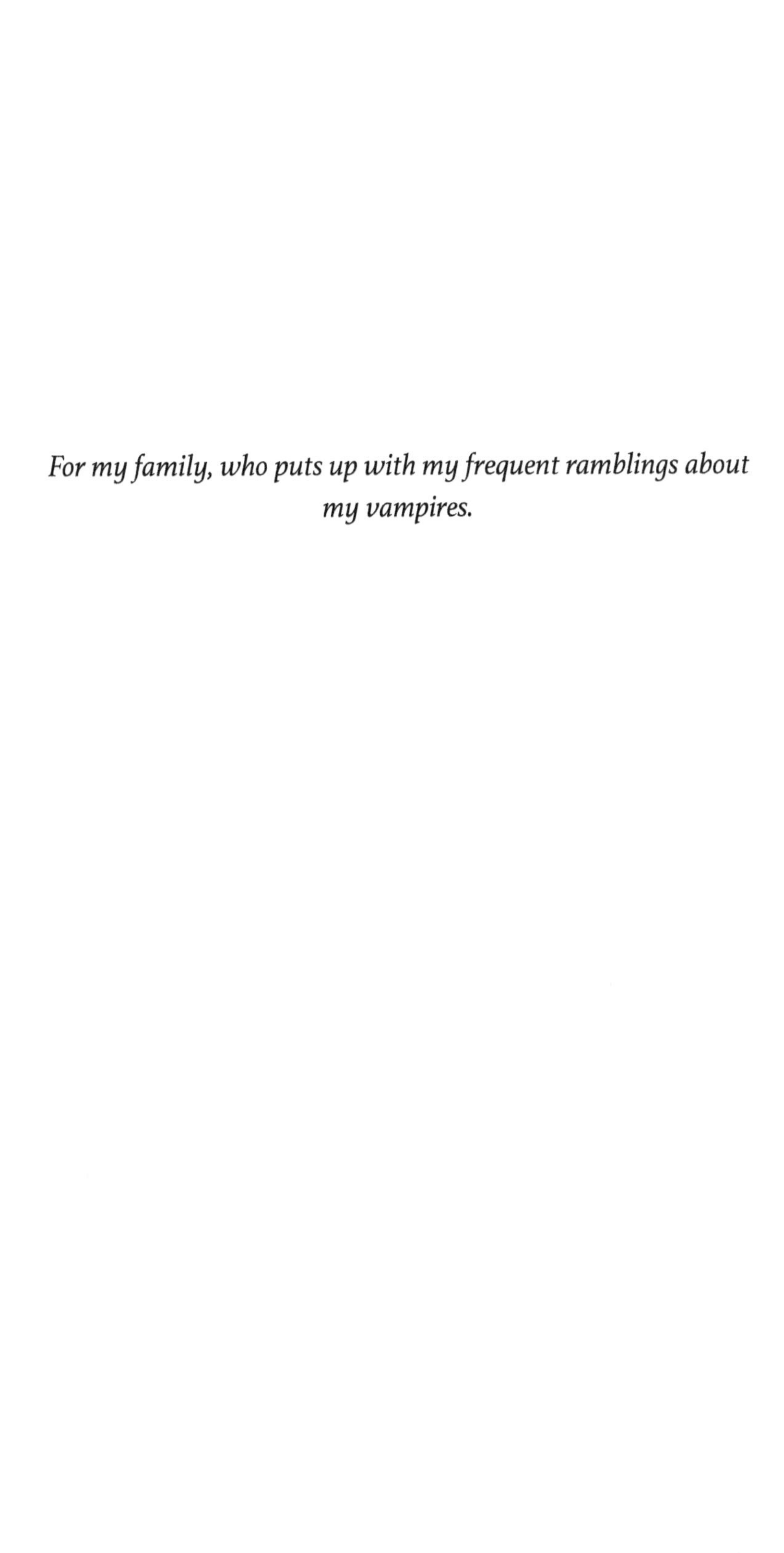

For my family, who puts up with my frequent ramblings about my vampires.

Auspicious
 Is it auspicious
 To run into a vampire
 During October?
 — Ramona Ridgewell, SciFaiku, 2024

VOLUME THREE: VAMPIRE HOUSE

1

SHARED HOUSING

May 1, 2020
Rix

I stand on the landing, forehead pressed to the door. On the far side, Maggie's breath comes in ragged gasps. "Dammit, Rix," she growls, thumping the door. I've never known her to be so angry, and feel awful for being the cause. Can she ever move past this? Her stomping feet fade away. Turning, I descend the stairs.

In my room—my former room—I slip my laptop into my backpack. The camping mat takes up a lot of the remaining space. I need to figure out a way to strap it to the outside, but no time tonight. I change into clean clothing, adding what I was wearing to a small pile on the closet floor. After tugging on a second t-shirt, I roll the rest into little cylinders, for a tighter fit with less wrinkles, and stack them like bricks, starting with a pair of jeans at the bottom, followed by my old hoodie, three t-shirts, and several pairs of underwear and socks. My toilet kit won't fit. When did I accumulate so much stuff? I fondle the tiny brown bottle of vanilla extract. It'll be expensive to replace, but I lay it on top of the toilet kit. My toothbrush, toothpaste and comb go loose into the pack. I force the zipper closed.

Ten minutes later, I'm outside, staring at a key too heavy to lift. I somehow manage to lock the door. Swallowing tears, I cross the backyard to the little fountain. Its burbling in the moss-covered hush calms me. I slip the reluctant key into the basin. It creeps slowly down, clinging to the rough granite, until it disappears beneath the ripples of the tiny cascade.

Pulling out my phone, I open the text app.

> Sorry I deceived you, Maggie. Never meant to hurt you. I hope you can forgive me. Key's in the fountain.

I scroll to Bryer's name.

> Need a place for the day.

After a lingering glance around the tranquil garden, I trudge from the yard on unwilling feet. Instead of making directly for Bryer's, I walk up Forty-fifth. If she doesn't respond by the time I get to the U-District, I'll head to Capitol Hill and track down James or Jewel. Or Robert.

As I wait for the light at Fremont Avenue, my phone vibrates.

> The more the merrier.

See you in a few.

When I arrive, Cleve opens the door. "Your old lady kicked you out, huh?" He smiles faintly, dropping a heavy hand on my shoulder. "You really do want to sleep in the park with me."

We join Bryer in the front room. "We're a little full at the moment, but the grand suite's still available." She waves her arm vaguely around the room, making the salmon tips of her spiked hair sway. "Take your pick. That one"—she points across the room—"is the most comfortable."

Poking at my sleeping mat, Cleve grins. "I see you came prepared."

"It helps with concrete basement floors." I set my pack on the floor, wedged between the couch Bryer indicated and a small rack of dumbbells.

"Where's your bedroll?" He chuckles, but when he sees my dour reaction, his face becomes somber.

"Settle in," Bryer says. "We'll find you a blanket and pillow."

By myself in the faint light of a single lamp, I drop heavily to the couch—as if my legs will no longer hold me—and rest my forehead in my hand. Cleve's arm around my shoulder causes my head to pop up. "I'm sorry what I said earlier." His deep voice is a booming whisper. "I'm no good with this stuff."

"I know you were teasing." We stand as Bryer walks in carrying sheets and a blanket, which she plops onto the couch. I force a smile. "Thanks. I can take it from here."

Going to the rack, she selects a pair of small weights.

When she sits on the adjacent couch, she begins flexing them.

Cleve sits beside her. "Did she figure out what she saw?"

While I consider how to answer his question, I fluff the pillow and tuck in the blanket. "Not exactly."

Bryer snorts. "What's that mean?"

"She thought I was cheating on her." I sit at the far end of my sofa, well away from Bryer. "With that man I was feeding on."

"Well, that's good." She sniggers. "So she kicked you out for being unfaithful."

"Or for being gay?" Cleve asks.

"Not really. Her mind kind of went there at first, and she was upset, but she was just looking for a monogamous relationship."

Bryer stops pumping in mid flex. All the frivolity leaves her. "Don't keep us in suspense." When I say nothing, embers stoke to life on her cheeks. "You didn't tell her."

"I can't lie to her."

Dropping the dumbbells, she leaps to her feet—her face a firestorm—and towers over me. "What the hell's wrong with you? You can't keep blaming all this on hunger. We're all hungry. Why did you choose to get involved with a *human*?" She spits out the final word.

"I didn't choose." I stare at my hands, tightly clenched in my lap. "I fell in love"—the words are barely audible—"for the first time since ..." With empty lungs that refuse to expand, I fall silent.

Cleve slips his arm around Bryer and guides her away,

murmuring in her ear, assuaging her. He's good at it, and good for her. He looks back at me from the doorway. "We'll talk later."

May 1, 2020
Corvina

"How're you feeling, girl?" A whispered voice pulls me from a strange dream. My head hurts. Pounds like a beating heart. A weight on my chest keeps me from taking a breath. I try to talk, but only moan. I open my eyes. The room's dim. Everything blurs. Spins. The pounding gets worse. My stomach's sick. I barf. "Close your eyes." A hand gently wipes puke from my cheek—as black and shiny as the rock on Jakob's necklace. I close my eyes. The spinning slows. "Frozen pig's blood isn't working," the voice mutters. "Sun's down. Dong Hing Market's open til nine. Just lay here. I'll be back soon."

I try to tell him not to go. No words. Sleep.

Bright light stabs my eyeballs right through my eyelids. I jerk awake. The man squats at the open mini-fridge door. I squint. In the glare, his big muscles move under a tight tee. He puts in some jars of strawberry soda—I love strawberry. His face is a weird brown. A long, dark ponytail hangs down his back. He's the man from my dream ... but there was something else. He shuts the door.

The room dims, but I can make out stacks of boxes and some garden tools. What is this place? A storeroom? He puts a jar in a microwave on the floor by the fridge. Starts it. Why's he heating strawberry soda? He wets a washrag from a water bottle. Turns to me. "I'm back." He wipes my face, my neck, my arms. The wet cloth feels good on my hot skin.

"Who ..." I croak.

"Shhh. Don't try to talk." His fingers are cool on my lips. "I'm Erlandr." The timer dinging sends needles poking through my brain. I flinch with each beep. He goes to the micro. Removes the jar. Holds it against his cheek—like Linda does with Kylie's bottle. He kneels beside me. Lifts my head.

"Ow." It pounds. I close my eyes.

"Drink." He holds the jar to my mouth. "This'll make you feel better." Thick liquid coats my tongue, salty and warm. I nearly gag. He pulls it away. "Just swallow a little." It oozes down my throat. Coats it like cough syrup. I open my mouth. He brings up the jar. I drink. My stomach settles. The drum in my head gets quieter. He sets the jar on the floor. Lowers my head to the wadded up t-shirt. "Let's see how you do now."

"Uh-huh," I grunt. Close my eyes.

I wake up. That giant weight's gone. I open my eyes.

Erlandr—I think that's what he said—sits beside me. "You look better."

I take a tiny breath. "Better," I murmur. "What happened"—I take another shallow breath—"to me?"

"When I found you, you couldn't breathe. You were burning with fever. Hallucinating. I tried to call nine one one, but my battery was dead. I sat with you. You quit breathing. Passed out. I had to do something." He runs a finger down my cheek. "Or just watch you die."

"I'm alive. Wha'd'ya do?" The more I talk, the easier it gets.

"Hard to explain. Well, not so hard to explain ... but you won't like it." He picks up the jar.

I drink. "What is this?"

He looks away. Makes a face. He's kind of cute. "You said, you're alive." He returns his brown eyes to me. "Not quite true. I couldn't keep you from dying. But I saved you."

I frown. My eyes flit across his face. Drop to the jar. "What's in that?"

"Blood."

"Shit! Wha'd'ya mean, blood?" I try to sit. Drop back to the cardboard.

"Don't be mad. If I left you, you'd be dead."

"How'd ya"—I choke on my words—"save me?"

"Turned you into a vampire." Sadness fills his face. "I'm sorry."

So Buffy wasn't crazy after all. "Ya shoulda asked me," I snarl, "if that's what I wanted." I squeeze my eyes shut. "What about my fam— my sister and Kylie? What do I tell my friends?"

He puts his cool hand on my cheek. I let him. Try to

calm myself. Open my eyes. He turns away. "You don't," he whispers. "I'm your family now. I'll take care of you."

May 2, 2020
Rix

I can't sleep. Maggie's shouted words, "I trusted you," repeat over and over in my mind. But for all the pain I've caused her—and me—I'm thankful for our time together. She made me feel like a person, worthy of affection, and offered me friendship. And unwarranted trust. Tears well in my eyes. Rolling to my side, I pull the pillow over my head to shut out the world, and finally fall asleep.

When someone pokes my shoulder, I spring over the back of the couch—along with my blanket—and land in a crouch on the floor. Peering around, I try to figure out where I am. I definitely don't recognize the goth woman leering at me from the other side of the couch.

"What are you supposed to be?" Contempt drips from her words, but her ashy cheeks hold no fire. The tattooed head of a bright blue bird peeks from under her tank top —black, in the same inky shade as her long, straight hair, and her mini skirt, leggings and boots.

"Um." Rising, I wrap the blanket around me and take in my surroundings. Last night's events come crashing back. "I'm Rix. Who are you?"

"Azul. ¿Qué estás haciendo aquí?" With her pale grey skin, accented to nearly white by makeup, I wouldn't have placed her as Latina—not that I pay much attention to that kind of detail—but her Spanish is as flawless as her English.

"Perdí mi lugar." My accent isn't nearly as authentic as hers. "Bryer let me sleep on the couch."

The frown on her charcoal lips curls up slightly, but her words remain harsh. "How long are you staying?"

"Aw, leave him alone." A voice from behind me makes me spin. "Gods, Rix, calm down."

"Shut up, David." Azul hisses.

"You shut up."

"Both of you shut up." Bryer enters from the other side of the room. Rolling his dark eyes, David retreats to the kitchen. Bryer turns her gaze on the young woman. "Azul, please be nice to our guest."

"Bienvenido a nuestra casa." She struts past me to follow David.

"And Rix, please get dressed." Sitting, Bryer sizes me up, like she's deciding if I'm worthy of her attention. "You're kinda skinny."

"I've always been lean." I pull on my t-shirt.

Cleve comes in. "You should feed more." He sits beside Bryer, slinging his arm around her shoulders. When she turns her head to smile at him, he kisses her. He's always full of kisses.

"And workout." She nods toward the dumbbell rack. "You can use my weights."

"Thanks for the kind offer." I sit to tug on my socks and shoes—they all wear shoes in the house. "I really appreciate you letting me stay here today." When my laces are tied, I sit back.

Bryer's attempted smile looks more like a grimace. "Don't do anything to make me throw you out."

Poking his head in from the kitchen, David announces, "Coffee's ready," then disappears again.

In the kitchen, Bryer tells him, "Go get Matt and Azul. House meeting."

Cleve pours me a cup of barely brown coffee. "It's kind of weak. We ran out of coffee. Do you want sugar?"

"No, um." Taking the cup, I peek into it. "Black?"

When we're all seated in the front room, Bryer clears her throat. "As you may have figured out, Rix moved in. I don't think he should sleep out here." She puts her focus on Matt and David. "At least for the short-term, is it OK if we set up the cot in your room?"

The corners of Matt's full lips tug down.

David's dark face glows his excitement. "That'll work for us." He gives me a boyish grin, making him appear even younger. "If we don't keep him awake."

"Matt?" Bryer's gaze is steely.

He studies David, whose eyes remain locked on me. "It'll be fine." He swigs the last of his coffee.

Azul stands. "Can I go now?"

"You can all go." Bryer has impressive control of this group.

David picks up my pack. "Grab your bedding."

"Careful." I reach for it. "My laptop's in there."

As he moves out of reach, he smiles. "Don't worry so much."

Staying in a vampire house again is going to be a challenge.

May 3, 2020
Corvina

"How're you doing today, Corvina?" Erlandr's voice is soft, as if he barely has enough air to make the words.

"I don't smell breakfast." My eyes blink open. "Keep hopin' I'll wake up in my own bed."

"You know that life's gone."

"Yeah. I know. I'm dead."

"Not dead," he says quickly, "just not exactly alive. Can you get up?"

"I dunno." I push myself to my elbows. My head spins. I collapse to the thick pile of cardboard. "Not really."

Brushing back my hair, Erlandr puts his hand on my forehead. He's so gentle. "The virus damaged you. You'd be stronger with human blood, but all I can bring is from pigs. I don't think you'll recover til you actually feed."

"I'm not doin' that." I look away. "Ever."

"We'll see." He gets to his feet. "Probably not tonight." Grabbing his backpack and black hoodie, he heads to the door. "We're outta blood. I'll see if they got any more at Dong Hing Market. Otherwise, I need to find it somewhere else." He reaches for a key on a hook, then pulls the door shut behind him. The lock clicks.

A rattle of the doorknob startles me awake. The room's pitch black. Outside, shoes scuff and fade away. Dragging myself to sitting, I wrap my arms around my knees and stare into the darkness toward where the door should be. I wait.

At the click of the lock, I try to get up, but drop back to the cardboard. The door opens. "Erlandr?" I whisper.

"It's me." Rushing in, he locks the door. As he turns, the light from his phone makes his face blueish white, and the shadows make his eyes into empty holes—like a creepy skull. "I'm glad you're up. Can you walk?"

When he comes closer and reaches a hand toward my forehead, I back away. "Don't touch me."

His hand drops. "We need to leave." He looks at his phone. "Right now. Can you stand?" The glare of the flashlight makes me squint. He finds my boots. "Put these on." After stuffing his things into a duffel bag, he zips it.

I get sick to my stomach and roll to my back. "I can't."

Erlandr pulls a small jar from his backpack. "Sorry, I can't heat this." After unscrewing the top, he lifts my head. "Drink just a little. It was the last jar they had." He holds it to my lips. "Then, we can go."

I sip. "Go where?"

After putting the jar in the pack, he slips his arms into the straps. "I don't know yet." He pushes my boots onto my feet, then helps me sit up and get my jacket on. "But I do know we can't stay here. They cut off the power I was stealing. This place is set for demolition. I just didn't think it'd start so soon." He holds my backpack as I get my arms through the straps, then pulls me to standing. "Let's go." As I cling to his backpack, he puts his arm around me and picks up his bag. We shuffle to the door. He peeks outside before we slip into the night.

May 3, 2020
Rix

Plopping to the couch, Bryer points beside her. "How'd you sleep?"

"Fine." I sit where she indicated. "But, it's unfair to Matt and David for me to sleep in their room."

"Don't worry about it. They chose to take the largest room."

"Regardless, I'm running up to Capitol Hill to look for my old roommate, James." I'm not excited about this decision, but I don't want to wear out my welcome here. "I haven't checked on him in a while." I shrug. "Maybe he's got more space."

"I thought you were staying away from him. Away from the Hill." Her expression turns dark. "Don't draw any of that chaos here."

"At least, I should check in on him. And see if they've had any other encounters with the ... abductors."

"That would be good to find out, but it's no reason to stay. We can fit you in here." She puts her hand on my arm. "Whatever you do, stay safe."

"I'll text if I decide to sleep somewhere else tonight. Otherwise, I'll see you later."

After the sun sets, I catch a bus out to Darah's to see if James moved back in with her. When I knock, the porch light comes on. A moment later, the door opens as far as the security chain allows. One dark eye peeks through the gap.

"Hey, Darah." I try to keep my voice friendly.

"What do you need?" Hers is not so friendly.

"Is James staying here?"

"I haven't seen him in a while. Did you try that place on Nineteenth?"

"Not yet." I smile. "Thanks."

The door shuts, the lock clicks and the light goes out. I head north, jogging over to the house with the perpetually blue-tarped roof. The basement door stands half open. I peek inside. After listening carefully, I slip down the hall and into the room where we slept. Completely empty. I sniff. No one's been here for a while. As much as I hate the prospect of staying with Robert, I continue northward in my search for James.

Stopping by the restaurant where he used to work, I loiter in the alley by the kitchen door until someone comes out to have a smoke. "Hey." I step from the shadows, causing the woman to nearly drop her cigarette. "Sorry. Didn't mean to startle you."

She coughs a laugh. "Take more than you to startle me." Clicking her lighter several times before a flame catches, she puffs on the cigarette until the end glows red.

"Busy tonight?"

"Only take out, with the virus, but very steady. This is my first break all evening." She sizes me up. "Do you need food?"

"No." I blink in surprise. "Thank you for the kind offer.

I'm looking for someone. You remember James, that guy who used to clean here?"

"That weird guy? Yeah." She coughs, takes a deep drag, blows out a halo of smoke. "I remember him."

"Have you seen him?"

"Not since he walked out. I wish Fernando'd quit taking in all the strays."

"Thanks."

I head to Cal Anderson Park. Tonight, the courtyard is set up as an impromptu skateboard park. The crowd that watches through the chainlink fencing is much smaller than the last time I was here, and nearly everyone wears a mask. Near the reservoir, I spot Jewel, scanning the crowd. When she notices me, her face ignites in a passionate ashy pink. We duck into a dark corner of the pump house.

"Where ya been hidin' yourself, Rix?"

"I'm still in Wallingford. Where are you staying? Are James and Dan with you?"

She rolls her eyes. "Yup. We're up near Volunteer Park, in another basement, even smaller than that last one, and just as damp. And there's six of us sharing four mats."

My gut clenches. "What happened?"

"I wasn't there. Somethin' about us bein' squatters. All our stuff was strewn out by the sidewalk, right where anyone could riffle through it. Not that we had a lot to riffle through. Even less, now."

"That's not good." At least, it wasn't a raid. Probably just a normal eviction? I relax—a little. "I'm sorry you keep going through this."

"Is there room for another body or two where you're stayin'?" She looks so optimistic, I hate to dash her hopes.

"Not really. I'm already in a room shared by two others." And I'm certain Bryer would throw me out if I bring any more vampires to the house. "I was hoping you all might have space for me."

She nods her sympathy. "Well, that's the life of folks like us. I should get back to hunting. Too many people here." As she walks away, she looks over her shoulder to give me a little smile.

May 3 to 4, 2020
Rix

Since I'm hungry, and there's no sign of Robert, I may as well go hunting on my way back to Bryer's. I dodge the numerous tents set up in the grassy areas of the park. Jewel is right. Way too many barely housed people mill around. I notice a couple sticking to the shadows along the fringes. Crossing the playfield, I start my pursuit. They move slowly. The smaller one leans heavily on the larger one—probably a man—who's loaded like a Sherpa, with two backpacks and a duffel bag. Are they homeless? I'm about to look elsewhere when he turns his head. Frowning, he tries to hurry his companion, who slumps to the ground. He spins to face me. Something's not right. He lacks the usual stupor of my potential victims. It's really hard to tell under the bright sidewalk lights, but his heat signature appears very cool.

He gives me a long look, equally surprised at my reaction, or rather, lack of reaction. "Who're you?" His voice is so soft, I strain to hear the words.

"A better question is why are you hunting in this territory? Did you get Robert's permission?"

He purses his lips, then ignores me to drop his burden and kneel beside his victim. After pulling a half-empty container of carmine liquid from a pack, he rolls her to her back. Scarlet blotches her ashen skin. She's a vampire, but something's wrong with her. "Drink some," the man murmurs.

I gawk. "What's going on?"

"She's sick." Barely audible. Maybe something's wrong with him, too.

I take a step back. "What do you mean, sick?"

"Actually, recovering ... from COVID." He puts the jar away.

"But isn't she ..." I sputter. "I didn't know we could ..."

"We can't. At least I don't think we can. It's complicated." He waits for her to open her eyes. "Right now, I need to find a safe place for her."

I pace in a circle until he gets her to her feet. I'm hungry, but I can't leave them here. "Come with me." I load myself with his bags.

The girl peers at me. "Hey." Her voice is faint, but her face fills with surprised recognition. "You're that guy. You bought me a Dick's burger."

I look more closely at the girl, her early teen face, her dark hair with a blue streak. "I remember you. Strawberry shake."

"Yep. What's your name?" she asks.

"My legal name's John, but I go by Rix."

"I don't have a legal name, but all my friends call me Corvina." She gives me a sleepy grin. "All my friends from"—her smile fades—"before." When she scrunches her forehead, she reminds me of my daughter, Eri, at the same age. "Are you a vampire, too?"

"Shh." I peer about, but no one seems to have heard her. I keep my voice at barely more than a whisper. "Yes, but we don't talk about that around"—I take another look over my shoulder—"regular people."

Her eyes grow large. "Oh. Sorry."

"No harm done." I turn a questioning expression on the man, who's younger than I first thought, maybe nineteen or twenty.

He finally meets my eyes. "I'm Erlandr."

"Foreigner?" I'm not certain where I've heard that. He nods once. I start walking. "We should get moving. We've got a ways to go before sunup."

Erlandr and I take turns, either helping Corvina to walk or carrying their bags. As we approach the University Bridge, the girl collapses. I carry her piggyback for the final two miles to Cleve and Bryer's. The coming sun paints the high, scattered clouds in flames of tangerine and lemon, as if the sky's on fire. I bump the door with my foot. Bryer peeks out. Her mouth drops open.

"May we come in?" I nod to the east. "The sun's coming up."

Her mouth closes and scrunches into a frown. Resigned, she opens the door and holds her hand out toward the front room. Lurching in, I awkwardly drop Corvina's limp body onto the first couch.

Behind me, I hear Erlandr's soft voice. "Thank you for

letting us stay. I don't know what I'd have done if Rix hadn't found us. Oh, I'm Erlandr."

"I'm Bryer." There was a hint of civility in that. "That's Cleve."

Cleve appears beside me with a pillow and helps get the girl situated. He whispers, "Bry doesn't like uninvited guests."

As we both stand, I look at him and shrug, then turn to face Bryer, with Erlandr hovering deferentially behind her. "I'm sorry. I should've texted first to ask." At her glare, I attempt an impish smile. "I was kind of busy. What was I supposed to do? Robert would've taken Corvina to prostitute her—can you imagine how popular she'd be?—and probably staked Erlandr."

The young vampire's brows shoot up, and fearful orange brushes his cheeks. Pursing her lips in disgust, Bryer leaves us. In a sudden flurry of motion, Cleve helps Erlandr move his bags between the first two couches. He grins at me. "I figured we'd want to keep your regular couch free, in case you need to sleep in here."

I glance over my shoulder at the two youths, then return my gaze to him. "What do I do now?" I mutter.

"Let's get them settled." He tries to keep his voice low. "Then, you and I should go talk to Bry."

We make up beds while Erlandr washes in the bathroom. After he returns and lies down, with his head near Corvina, I touch his shoulder. "You'll be safe here," I murmur.

He glances up with weary eyes. "Thanks, Rix."

Cleve leads me down the hall into a dimly lit bedroom containing only a queen bed wedged into the far corner, a tall, skinny dresser, and another, larger weight set. Vampire strength isn't enough, I guess. No wonder Bryer's so muscular. Cleve, too. Maybe I *should* work out, put on some muscle, but that would require feeding more often. Bryer sits with her back against the headboard, flexing a small dumbbell with one hand. Looking up from her phone, she scowls at me and goes back to scrolling.

After closing the door behind us, Cleve sits against the wall at the foot of the bed. He pats the space between himself and Bryer. "Have a seat."

I push off my shoes and crawl onto the bed. As soon as my back touches the wall, Bryer's head comes up. "What the hell, Rix?" Her softly glowing cheeks don't match the harshness of her voice.

When my hands ball, regardless, Cleve takes the closest one and gives a little squeeze. I glance at him. As usual, he remains totally calm. I shake off his hand, draw my knees up to my chest and return my gaze to Bryer. "Would you have left them to Robert?"

Bryer's eyes dart from me to Cleve, but land back on me. "Probably not." Her frown's sullen. "You brought them. You're responsible for them." She holds my gaze. "Good luck with the kid." Thumbing open her phone, she dives back into the internet.

After putting his arm around me, Cleve pulls me close to whisper in my ear, "Don't worry. We'll help." He leaves his arm in place. "Why don't you sleep in here tonight?"

My brows rise. Is he hitting on me? I thought he and Bryer were a couple. "All three of us?" With a shy smile he nods, but his cheeks hold no passion. Can he hide that? "I ... I'm flattered," I stammer, "but ..."

"Mmm. You smell good." He softly kisses my cheek. "Just sleep."

May 4, 2020
Rix

I stir in my sleep—too hot. My brother, Gareth, who lies beside me, is red with fever. He coughs and coughs. The sheet under us is wet. On his other side, Alan moans a rasping croak. I sit up. My head pounds. Where's Mama? She's lying across the foot of the bed. Oh, no! Did I let her die? "Mama?" I whisper, as I crawl to her.

"There's my boy," she wheezes. "Go heat some of the tea I made with the herbs. We all need some."

I slip onto the cold floor. My damp nightshirt clings to my back, making me shiver. I pull on a sweater and stuff my feet into my shoes. Not supposed to wear shoes in the house. In the main room, the stove is cold. I've never made the fire by myself before. How will I heat the tea?

My body shudders. I struggle to pull myself awake. Where *am* I? I inhale the scent of two vaguely familiar people. Very close to me. Not my brothers, nor my mother. Forcing my eyes open, I tilt my head slightly left and right. Enough light leaks around the blind for me to make out Bryer and Cleve. I can't believe I let him talk me into sleeping with them.

Cleve turns toward me, onto his side, and drapes his thick arm across my chest. When I roll away, he snugs against my back. Moving his arm off me, I scoot to sitting

—at least, I'm wearing my boxers—and crawl from under the blankets to the foot of the bed. He paws at the empty space I left behind. "Where'd you go, Bry?" he murmurs.

"Right here." She scoots toward him.

As they entwine themselves around each other, I pull my phone from the pocket of my jeans. Eleven-thirty. Gathering my clothing and shoes, I pad quietly out to the front room. My couch squeaks as I lie down. Erlandr shifts, but doesn't awaken.

I n the belly of the stove, I stack a little pile of kindling on top of some shavings, then strike the blade against the flint, like Alan showed me. It takes many tries, but finally a spark jumps from the knife to the tinder. I gently blow on the growing flames. Smoke comes out. I jump up to open the damper. I always forget that part. After adding wood to the growing fire and closing the door, I put the kettle of tea on top and sit on the cold floor to wait. My eyelids droop shut.

At a bang, I'm sitting, eyes wide. In the kitchen, David whispers, "Quiet. You'll wake the dead." His head appears in the doorway. His cheeks glow passionate pink when he spots me. "Sorry. Matt's a klutz."

Rubbing my face, I murmur, "What time is it?"

Matt nuzzles David's neck and pokes his head around his shoulder. "Four-thirty. And I'm not a klutz."

"But look who woke up." David smirks. "When you slept out here, we worried you didn't like us anymore."

"Ha ha." Dropping my feet to the floor, I grab my jeans. "I should be up anyway."

On the next couch, Erlandr jerks upright and peers around. "Good morning." He stretches and tries to scratch an out-of-reach itch between his shoulder blades. By the time I set my folded blanket in a corner at the end of the couch, he's dressed and perched beside Corvina. Folding his bedding, I set it on top of mine. He looks up, brow creased. "I wonder if she'll wake up again."

"Only time will tell." I sit on the adjacent couch. "Probably." When Matt and David enter, I get up. Erlandr stands to face them. I point at the larger ashy-faced blond. "This is Matt, and that"—I indicate the lithe younger man —"is David. This is Erlandr."

David's dark face carries a peach glow as he runs his eyes over me before turning to Erlandr, who just stares. He steps forward to offer his hand. "Nice to meet you."

Erlandr doesn't so much shake it, as give it a gentle squeeze. "Likewise." Barely a whisper, as if he never really figured out how to breathe. Some vampires never do. It's not like we need to, except to speak and smell things.

Staying put behind David, Matt gives a bored little wave. "Me, too." He nods toward Corvina with his chin. "What's up with her?"

At Erlandr's silence, I say, "She's never fed."

David's brows shoot up. "That sucks."

"I got a couple of midnight snacks in the fridge," Matt says to Erlandr, "for your girl. They're fresh and need to get used soon, anyway. Just replace them when you can."

"Thanks," Erlandr murmurs, then sits and puts his focus on Corvina.

"Azul won't like sharing." David's eyes rapidly dart as he thinks. "If you didn't notice, she's very antisocial."

"Bryer hates that she won't hunt with a partner," Matt pipes in.

"Rix is just as bad," Bryer mutters as she pads into the room, wearing a tight-fitting tank and sports shorts that show off her well-muscled body. Cleve trails right behind her.

"Sorry we woke you." Matt wraps his arms around David. "We were just chatting about accommodations."

"Cleve's giving up his room to move in with me." She eyes me up and down. "Unless you two want to share."

"Um …" I look at him, abashed. "I'll just sleep on the cot."

"He'll be disappointed, won't you honey?" She nudges him in the ribs. When he only silently smiles, I squirm. She can't hold back a grin. "You're too easy to tease."

Azul clomps in, wearing thick-soled shiny black Doc Martens. "Oh. So you *are* back." Her eyes brush past me, landing on Erlandr. A smile tugs at her lips, and her voice becomes much more amiable. Friendly, even. "Hi. I'm Azul."

"Erlandr."

Bryer crosses her arms, turning her focus on Azul. "Someone needs to sleep with you."

She doesn't hesitate. "I'll take Erlandr. I'm certainly not sharing my bed with Rix."

Bryer sets her gaze on him. "Are you OK with that?" At his nod, she smiles. "All right, then. Corvina gets her own room. Welcome to the family, at least for now."

"We'd better get some blood into that kid." Azul tugs

Erlandr toward the kitchen. "Then, let's get you smelling better."

"As soon as my bedding's washed"—with his arms full of sheets, Cleve points with his chin at Corvina—"we can move her into my room."

"I'm going to shower before all the hot water's gone." Bryer rises. As she exits, she mutters, "I wonder if we have enough towels to go around."

"Don't pay attention to her." Cleve drops the sheets and lays his hand on my shoulder. "She just likes to grump. We'll get everyone settled in."

Erlandr returns, alone, with the jar. Sitting beside Corvina, he tenderly strokes her cheek. "Wake up, Corvina." She murmurs something incoherent. He doesn't give up. "I got something for you. I'll help you drink it." He lifts her head, but it rolls forward, with her chin resting between her clavicles.

"She's doing worse than anyone I've seen when they first transition. Being sick must have really weakened her." I grab a pillow and tuck it under her shoulders, then cradle her head. "Try now."

Holding the rim to her mouth, Erlandr carefully tips the jar until a tiny bit of the warm liquid wets her lips, then lifts it away. Her tongue peeks out to lick it off.

"More," Corvina softly grunts. After a few sips, her eyes flutter open. She lifts her hand to cover Erlandr's, then pulls the jar to her mouth, takes a swallow and pushes it away. Blinking, she focuses on Erlandr. "More." After another swallow, she slumps back.

I slip out my hands. At least three-quarters of the container remains. "She didn't drink enough." Looking over my shoulder, I meet Cleve's eyes. "Hand me another pillow?"

Erlandr sets down the jar to help me wedge the pillows more comfortably behind Corvina. "How's that?" he asks. When she nods, he picks up the container. "Want to try some more?"

"Yeah."

I sit beside Cleve while Erlandr feeds the girl. When she finishes, her face holds more color.

"Rest now," Erlandr coos. "We'll move you into a room in a bit, so you can have a little privacy." Rising, he turns to me. "Will you watch her? I'm going to see if I could take a shower."

"No problem."

Before he's through the door, Cleve rises. "I'll go check on Bry."

The front room's quiet for the first time since I woke up. When my head bobs, I move to the end of the couch closest to Corvina, and rest it back. Although uncomfortable, I'm really tired. I close my eyes, but I can't nap. Too many sounds fill the house: Bryer and Cleve's murmurs from her room down the hall; laundry running; the steady, soft squeak of sex; a moan; a giggle; the splash of a shower.

"Rix?" Corvina's soft voice brings me immediately alert.

"What is it?" I move to sit beside her on the edge of the cushion.

"Just makin' sure it's you." She looks away from me. "Why am I here?"

"Erlandr and I brought you. You two lost your place."

"Yeah, I know that." Her eyes return to me. "I should be dead. Why am I here?"

"Oh." What can I say? "Erlandr has a gentle spirit. He couldn't watch you die."

"Now what?"

"You adapt, and do your best to survive. When you're strong enough, I'll teach you to hunt."

She shakes her head and closes her eyes. "I'm tired."

I go back to my couch.

After way too long to take a shower, Erlandr returns, carrying clean bedding. "I'll make up her bed. Then, can you help me move her?"

When Corvina's settled, we close the door and retreat to the front room, where Azul's waiting.

"Oh, I forgot to tell you." Erlandr's voice drops to nothing more than a whisper. "Azul's going to take me hunting, show me around the neighborhood. I haven't fed in days. Can you watch Corvina?"

My stomach gurgles, but I should work. Now's as good a time as any. "Please, don't stay out too late. I need to feed, too."

"We'll do our best." Azul shrugs. "But you know how things are."

I head downstairs to retrieve my laptop. Outside the door, I stop to listen.

"Mm, David," Matt grunts, "that feels so good."

No work for now. I'll try to get some sleep upstairs.

2

TEENAGERS

May 4, 2020
Corvina

The door creaks.

"Go away." Way too loud. I stuff my things under the covers and put my hand over my other wrist. Rix's head pokes in. "Wha'd'ya want?" I scowl.

He opens the door and comes in, like he owns the place. "I told Erlandr I'd look in on you." Pulling a chair from the corner, he sits by the bed. His eyes go from my face to my hand. "I thought you were asleep. What's going on?"

"I woke up." I shimmy my butt closer to the wall. It's hard, not using either hand.

Rix moves to the bed and reaches toward me. "What happened?" When I pull my hands against my chest, he moves even closer. "Let me see." His eyes come up to mine. "Please?"

Lowering my arms, I remove my hand. "Not much blood." I poke at the gaping wound with a finger.

"Here." Grabbing my wrist, he leans in. "Let me take a look." He pushes the sides together with his thumb and finger. How long's he going to do this for? Finally, he frowns and says, "Hold that. I'll be right back."

As I wait, I fidget with the cut. The small amount of dark, red blood barely lets the skin slide, and it doesn't run—like the last time—but stays close to the slit. When I smear it with my finger, it reminds me of fudge syrup, but not as sticky. It does *not* provide the pain I wanted.

Rix comes back, carrying a tiny suitcase, like my old Buffy lunchbox. "Stop that," he says, and drags the chair closer. Popping the latches, he lifts the lid. The alcohol smell of the ER comes out. I crinkle my nose. He glances at me. "If you don't like the odor"—he chuckles—"we don't need to breathe." We don't? After setting the box on the bed, he snaps on a pair of gloves and takes my arm. "You can let go now."

I lean against the wall and watch him clean the cut. When the alcohol hits it, I jerk my arm, but he holds on too tight. "Ow," I whine. I wanted sharp, take-your-breath-away pain, not stinging.

"Sorry." He doesn't even try to make it sound like he means it. When the blood's gone, he looks close at my arm before setting it on his thigh. He opens a pack of Steri-Strips and peels off part of the back. Using the flat tip of a funny-looking pair of tweezers, he sticks it to the end of the strip and pulls off the rest. The strip wiggles like a nightcrawler before he lowers it. Holding it with a finger, he pulls it to the other side of the cut. Just like the nurse at the ER.

"You're pretty good. Are ya a doctor?"

He smiles a little. Why's he so nice? "I've been an EMT." He lays two more strips across the wound and two along the sides. "When did you start cutting yourself?"

"I dunno." When did Buddy move in? I press my lips together. I don't want to talk about that.

After putting a pad over the strips—bright white next to my weird greyish skin—he wraps the whole thing in a stretchy band, then moves my arm to my lap. He latches the box shut and grabs the trash. The scraps disappear inside the glove as he tugs it off. He covers everything with the other glove, making a little ball. When he tosses it at the trash can by the door, it bounces off the rim and lands a few inches beyond it. He looks at me. "How's your arm? Is the bandage too snug?"

I poke at the edges to give me something besides Rix to focus on. "It's OK."

"Don't mess with it."

"Why'd ya stop me?" When he doesn't say nothing, I look up. He's still watching. "Why ya so nice to me? I thought you're supposed to be a monster." This makes him look away. I feel smug. I want to hurt someone.

"Listen." He turns back to me and looks in my eyes. "We're only monsters if we *choose* to be. And I choose *not* to be."

"But ya are. And now I am, too. Why'd Erlandr do this to me?" Tears sting my eyes. I wipe them angrily away with the back of my hand. "Why'd you?"

"What did I do?"

"I'd just plain be dead now, if it wasn't for you. I was so tired of bein' hungry, and ya fed me. That boy woulda ..." I choke, with tears streaming down my cheeks. "He woulda ..." Just like Buddy did. As I sob, snot runs from my nose. Rix hands me a tissue. "Ya stopped him. You were nice to me. I was gonna kill myself, and you gave me *hope*, and then"—my voice cracks, so I whisper—"I couldn't." Rix scoots onto the bed. When he takes my hand, I jerk it away. "Don't," I growl. "This is all your fault. If I was dead, I wouldn'a got sick. Erlandr wouldn'a found me." I glare at him. "I wouldn't be a monster. *Why* were ya nice to me?"

"Maybe"—he talks so soft I have to lean forward to hear him—"it's because I had a daughter ... once upon a time. She was about your age when ... when what happened to you, happened to me. I still miss her. That night we first met, all I could think about was, what if this was *my* daughter, out on the street alone. So, you're right. I *am* a monster. I was only thinking of myself—of her. It wasn't about you." He hands me another tissue. "I should have made it about you. Done something besides buy you a burger. Found a safe place for you. And for that, I'm truly sorry."

I blow my nose. "I woulda run."

He nods. "I need to explain some things to you. You pretty much can't kill yourself. Cutting your wrist just makes a mess." His eyes go to my bandaged arm, then move back up to mine. "We don't metabolize pills the same way that humans do, so that probably won't work. Maybe a gun to the head, but that would hurt—a lot— and you'll just end up stupid." He moves back to the chair.

"Then, you'll kill people. I don't think you want to do that."

"Have *you* killed anyone?" I croak, my eyes wide.

"Not by choice," he whispers. "It was a long time ago."

"That's *never* gonna happen to me." I hug my knees to my chest. "I'm never gonna bite no one."

"That's not really an option." His face is sad. "You'll get weak. Way weaker than you already are. You'll be hungry all the time. You may go insane, but you won't die."

I don't want to hear that. I rest my forehead on my arms. My eyes burn again with tears. When Rix puts his hand on my shoulder, I look up.

"Why don't you lie down and rest until Erlandr gets back." He covers me, like Linda used to do. I miss Linda. And Kylie. "I'll come check on you in a while." After grabbing his medical kit, he stoops by the door to pick up the wad of gloves and drops it in the trash. The latch softly clicks as he pulls the door shut.

I haven't felt so alone since the night I left home.

May 4, 2020
Rix

Staring at my computer screen, I tap my fingers lightly on the keys, too distracted to concentrate. I'm happy Corvina's still sleeping. I don't want to have to patch her up again, so I decided to work in here. At least, that's what I told myself I'd do. When'll Erlandr be back? I need to feed, too. Maybe my hunger impacted my ability to heal the girl. Or maybe vampires can't heal each other. I've never tried to do that before. At any rate, we can heal ourselves, so she should be fine. I stand, setting my machine on the chair.

After pacing the few steps to the door and back a couple of times, I stop by the bed. Corvina doesn't so much bring up longing for my past life, as remembering. I haven't thought about my family for such a long time. Let the past be the past. How long ago was that? My wife's dead, but my girl could still be living—she was the last time I checked—although she'd be around ninety. Wow, I would've turned a hundred and ten on my last birthday. If I still had birthdays. Glancing at the laptop, I toy with the idea of googling her name.

A rattle of the outside door interrupts my thoughts. I check my phone—nearly three-thirty. Too late to hunt. I'm so ready for the nights to get longer, and we're not even to the solstice yet. A moment later, Erlandr enters. Swinging the door with his foot, he quietly bumps it closed. In the amber light of the single lamp, his cheeks appear flushed. A smear of blood stains his chin.

"Successful hunt?" I ask.

Jars clink as he un-shoulders his backpack. When he moves to put it on the chair, I snatch my laptop. After unzipping the pack, he withdraws three pint jars of blood, setting them on the nightstand. "This is all the pig's blood they had." He pulls out two smaller containers and sets them beside the trio.

"What are those?"

"Other kinds of blood. Sheep and cow, I think. Azul's

idea. She was willing to pay, so I didn't argue. It needs to be refrigerated."

"Of course. What are they for?"

"To pay back Matt? If he wants it. It's really hard to find fresh pig's blood, and Corvina couldn't tolerate frozen." He screws up his nose. "When we run out, I guess we can try those." He frowns at the bandage on her arm. "What happened?"

"She cut herself."

"How bad? Did *you* bandage her? It looks professional."

"I have some medical training."

"I thought you were watching her." His cheeks flare, then immediately fade.

"She was sleeping. Something came up at work. I needed to be on a call. I do need to work or I can't pay our rent."

"Oh. I didn't think about rent." He looks abashed. "Is she all right?"

"Physically, she'll be fine in a few days. Mentally, your guess is as good as mine. She's too young to be a vampire, and she wasn't entirely stable before. She has scars from previous cuts." The tension in my voice rises. "I really don't know what you were thinking, with such a young girl."

Erlandr's face remains cool and his voice calm. "I had no choice."

"You always have a choice," I shoot back.

A blush of heat touches his cheeks, then fades. "You weren't there."

"Let's not argue in here. It doesn't change anything."

"What do we do now?"

I want to say, 'Why are you asking me?' but hold my tongue. Dealing with a hurting child stirred up emotions that toy with my head. Being tired and hungry isn't helping. I'm cranky. I'd like to go back to being alone in Maggie's basement. "Teach her to survive. First, she needs to feed."

"She said she won't."

"She told me that, too. Maybe if we all go out together, she'll want to feed if she sees me feeding, since you fed tonight. Maybe tomorrow night." What did I say? Except for my victims, who don't remember anyway, I've only ever fed in front of Cleve and Bryer—and that was purely because she insisted.

"How'd you know I fed?"

"Besides the blood on your chin?" I smirk. "You look ... healthier."

"I feel better." After glancing at the girl, Erlandr turns back to me. "How're *you* doing?"

"There's no time left to hunt tonight." I shake my head. "I still have some loose ends to tie up at work." Giving my computer a pat, I head for the door. "I'm trying to avoid the next round of layoffs. I'll be in the front room. Don't forget to put those jars in the icebox." When he looks perplexed, I add, "Refrigerator."

May 5, 2020
Corvina

"Wake up." Erlandr shakes my shoulder. "Rix wants to take us hunting."

Rolling away, I pull the blanket over my head. "Just bring me some blood."

"C'mon. He's waiting."

"I don't care. I don't wanna go."

"Corvina." What's Rix doing in my room? "Let's go."

I spin to sitting. It's cool how fast I can move, but it makes my stomach sick. "I don't wanna," I snarl.

"I can't make you feed." How's he stay so calm? "But I want you to see how it's done. Besides, it'll be good for you to get out of this room for a while."

"Oh, all right," I snap. "Git out, so I can git dressed."

"Don't forget your mask."

Outside, Erlandr walks ahead of me, but Rix stays right by my side. He keeps looking over, and I think he might take my arm. I *am* pretty weak. Erlandr's already half a block ahead.

"Erlandr," Rix calls softly.

Looking over his shoulder, Erlandr slows til we catch up. "Sorry. Wasn't paying attention."

At the corner, we turn left. Up ahead a couple of blocks, there's lots of trees. "We're actually goin' huntin'?"

Rix points with his chin. "That's Woodland Park. Where we're going. See?" His eyes crinkle, so he must be smiling behind his mask. "Not far."

After crossing the street, we follow a path into the woods. It's quiet. And dark, but I can see just fine. We start down a hill. I hear the thud of shoes on the dirt trail. A man appears from around a bend, breathing heavy as he jogs up toward us. We stop, and Rix pulls me behind a big tree. When Erlandr peers at him, Rix whispers, "Show me how you hunt."

Erlandr hides with us til the man, who slowed to walking, passes. He dashes after him.

Taking off behind him, Rix grabs his sleeve and tugs him back to me. "What're you doing?" he hisses. He can be a real jerk. Erlandr's embarrassed. Rix turns to me. "You don't chase them."

"Then, what do you do?" Erlandr's expression jumps from confusion to hurt.

I look back and forth between them. The excitement of coming outside wore off. And I don't want to hear Rix lecture. "I'm tired. Let's go back."

They both stare at me.

"No." Rix shakes his head. "Let *me* show you. You both need to learn this." He trudges off down the trail. When he spots another runner pause to stretch at one of the big Doug firs, he holds up a hand. "Stay here until I call for you." He strolls up to the guy, who's maybe five or six years older than me. "Hey. How are you doing?"

The man cocks his head toward him. "Fine." He goes back to stretching. When Rix is close enough to touch him, he looks up. "What do you want?"

"I'd like to introduce you to a friend." Rix puts his palm on the man's cheek. He just stares at him. Over his shoulder, Rix softly calls, "Come on down."

I glance up at Erlandr, then clomp over to Rix—who has fangs! "When'd ya git fangs?"

"Shh. Focuth on him." He turns back to the man. "Just relax," he coos. "You'll be fine." The man looks stoned. To me, Rix says, "Put your hand on hith neck."

When I squeeze between them, the man's body beats against my chest. He's downhill from me, so his neck's right there. My stomach growls. Rix waits for me to get my hand in place before letting go of the man's cheek. He stays pressed against my back. My hand gets hot. It's amazing. I can feel the blood pulsing. "Ow. I bit my tongue."

"You're doing fine," he whispers. "Slide your hand down. Right where it was, that's where you want to bite."

"I don't think I can do thith."

"I won't let anything bad happen."

All I want to do is bite this guy. Closing my eyes, I push my teeth into his neck. Nothing happens. This is a waste.

Rix's cheek touches mine. "Now, pull out just enough to let it flow."

When I do, hot thick liquid fills my mouth. I swallow. And swallow. And swallow. As I drink, I moan, or maybe it's the man. I dunno. My entire world shrinks to my mouth on his neck.

"That's enough," Rix murmurs in my ear. "Let him go." Ignoring him, I press harder. More blood flows. My constant hunger's finally going away. I don't want to quit. "Stop"—he wraps an arm around my shoulders—"or you'll kill him." When he takes a step back, I let him drag me along. As soon as my mouth comes away from the man's neck, Rix covers the bite with his hand. "Put your hand here."

"Why?" I growl, squirming to get away. I'm angry he made me stop. Now he wants me to stay here.

"Just do as I say. You need to stop the bleeding. Like I said, we don't want him to die." When I reach up my hand, Rix covers it with his. "Put steady pressure on it. Think about closing the wound."

My hand tingles. "That's weird." I try to pull it away to take a look, but Rix presses it too hard.

"Wait a bit longer." After what seems like *forever*, he lifts his hand from mine. "That should be enough."

"Good." I peel my hand away, the blood from the skin making it sticky. Where's the bite? "It's gone!"

"Quiet. Clean your hands and mouth with this." Rix hands me a wet cloth. "Now, wipe his neck." When I back away, he opens another packet and washes the man's neck some more. He puts his hand back on his cheek. "How're you feeling?"

The man blinks at Rix. "What happened?"

"You fell and scratched open your neck. I tried to clean it up for you." He waves the bloody cloth. "You should be more careful. These trails can be treacherous in this flat light."

The man staggers a little as he jogs away.

"That was amazing." Erlandr joins us. "Where'd you learn to do that?"

"What else would you do?" Rix sneers. "What do you do?"

"After biting them, I run away."

"How do you know if they're all right?"

"I only take a little." Erlander looks at the ground. "I'm afraid if I don't leave, I'll get caught."

"How do you know if you've killed anyone?" Rix almost shouts, then takes a quick look around. "We should get moving. Come on."

No one says a word on our walk back. Before I go into my room, Rix pulls a package from his pocket. "I nearly forgot." He hands it to me.

"It's a book." I make a face. He looks sad. I guess I should be nicer.

"It's about warrior cats." He tries to smile. "I thought it would give you something to fill your time."

"Thanks." I put on my friendliest smile, then go inside my room and close the door.

Stripping to my t-shirt, I slide under the covers. I feel warm, and my hunger's gone, for the first time since ... since I left home. Near the door, Rix and Erlandr whisper, but I can't make out their words. I drift into a dreamy sleep.

May 5, 2020
Rix

"You sired her," I hiss, mad, or disgusted, or just far too hungry. Watching Corvina feed was really difficult.

"Quiet," Erlandr murmurs. "I don't want you to upset her."

I tone down my voice to something less ... threatening. "You're meant to teach her how to be a good vampire. Sneaking up on victims is not being a good one. It's being a pretty shitty one." The volume of my voice rises. I really need some blood. I temper myself. "Where'd you learn to be a vampire, anyway?"

Erlandr's voice grows even softer. "I had to figure it out on my own."

"Oh." I blink in surprise. "That must've been difficult. How long have you been at it?"

"Not even two years." He leans against the wall. "I aged out of foster care. Was trying to get back home ... when it happened."

"I'm sorry you went through that." I put on a more sympathetic expression, which unexpectedly calms me. "I apologize for raising my voice. It's just that I'm so hungry, all the time."

"We all are." Erlandr's eyes drift, then land back on mine. "How about you? How long ago?"

"Longer than two years. Around seventy-five. The beginning's the hardest."

"I make lots of mistakes. I know that. I didn't think about the future with Corvina. She was so sick and alone, I had to do something."

"She'll be caught in that place between being a child and an adult—forever. You'll need to look after her. It's a big responsibility."

"I'm starting to understand." Erlandr's brows rise questioningly. "Will you teach me to hunt properly? Azul's not very good at it."

"All right. We don't want you killing anyone."

"I don't know if I have. Didn't mean to, if I did. Never stuck around long enough to find out. This is the longest I stayed anywhere." His sad expression makes him look terribly young. "I'm so tired of constantly running. And being alone." He slides his hand over his head to push stray hairs from his face. "I miss Ireland and the heather … and Mhamó. But I don't know if I should go there. And now, I have Corvina to look after."

"I know what you mean." My thoughts go to Maggie. "I found someone special, but I messed it up. I'd like to go back and fix it."

"If you spend some time hunting with me and Corvina, and maybe teach us some other"—he smirks—"*life skills*, we'll move on as soon as she's well enough."

"We can talk about that when the time comes. Let's get her healthier first." I study him. "How are you? Are you getting sick?"

"No. Just hungry. I didn't feed much last night." He smiles shyly. "Azul's too distracting."

"Tomorrow night, I'll take you hunting." My stomach growls. I don't know when I'll get to feed. "We should take Corvina along, to reinforce what I showed her tonight."

"Thanks." He meets my eyes. "I really appreciate it."

I nod. "I need to go work. Try to keep my job." I smile at him. "So we can afford the rent."

May 7 to 9, 2020
Rix

Late in the afternoon, I check on Corvina. When I rap on the door, Erlandr answers, "Come in." He's sitting on the bed, attentively watching her sip from a jar of blood. I close the door behind me and wait until he takes the container from her and sets it on the floor.

Crossing the room, I stand beside him and peer down at the girl. "How're you feeling today?"

She stares back with lifeless eyes. "Dead."

I exchange glances with Erlandr. When he stands, I take his place. "Is the blood making you stronger?"

"I guess." Her gaze wanders. "But now I'm so bored."

"I may be able to get a phone for you." I draw my knee up so I can face her more easily. Her eyes snap to mine, and she stifles a squeal. A smile tugs the corners of my mouth. "Would that make you less bored?"

"Please please please, Rix. I need a phone so bad."

"Let me see if I can afford it." I'm strapped for cash again, since I paid Maggie for May and also paid for three shares in this house, but I should be able to find a refurbished iPhone 6 or 8 for less than two hundred dollars.

I do a search. Walmart has them in stock. They offer free two-day delivery—maybe due to COVID restrictions —on the iPhone 8. I don't want my cash card tied to this address, so I use my new one at Ballard Mailbox. It's so much easier to get to than the Hill, and I no longer risk running into James.

Two nights later, I hike down to Ballard. I'm hungry, and alone for a change. After picking up the small package, which luckily fit in my box, I take the long way back to Bryer's, through Old Ballard and past Fred Meyer, then to Upper Fremont—just a block away from Maggie's. I resist the urge to walk down her street. I get all the way to upper Woodland Park before I find a lone person and enough privacy to feed.

When I get back to Bryer's, Corvina, with cheeks softly shimmering, surprises me at the door. "Did ya git it?"

"Yes." I slip off my pack. "But I still need to set it up for you."

"OK." Although she keeps her voice and expression hopeful, her disappointment's apparent in the fading glow from her cheeks.

If Matt and David are out hunting, I'll work on my cot. They're not in the room, but Erlandr and Azul are definitely next door, noisily pleasuring each other. Why aren't they out hunting, too? I drop onto the cot. At least, Apple makes the setup easy and quick. An hour later, I gather the phone's earbuds, cables and cords, and head upstairs.

Nestled in the corner of a couch, Corvina looks up from her book—she's actually reading—and drops it to her lap. I smile and sit next to her. "The phone's ready."

"Savage!"

When she reaches for it, I hold it back. "You have to make me some promises. You can't use this to talk to anyone you used to know. It's too dangerous—for you, as well as the rest of the house. I set it up so you can call or text me, Erlandr and Bryer, but that's it." Her eyes stay locked on the phone. Slipping it into my pocket, I wait for her to look up at me. "This is really important. You can use it for games, music and videos, but you can't use it for social media, or to call or chat with anyone. I locked those features. You'll need me to download anything."

She makes a moue and studies her hands. "All right." Bringing her eyes up to mine, she murmurs, "I promise. Can I have it now?"

Once the phone's in her hands, she dashes to her

room and closes the door, abandoning the warrior cats to the front room floor.

May 10, 2020
Maggie

What do you know? I take the day off and the temperature is forecast in the high eighties. I wish it wasn't quite so hot. With no one to talk to, I doom-scroll while I eat my breakfast. Wow. The unemployment rate hit fourteen-point-seven percent. And the COVID numbers are mind-blowing. Yesterday there were more than twenty-seven thousand new cases, just in America. As New York City begins to recover, the death toll has dropped to under fifteen hundred a day, still an unbelievable toll. And the government can't even figure out how to ship remdesivir to the places that could use it most. How will we ever survive this year? And how will my yard, with my lack of attention on top of the dearth of rain? I'd better get out there and see the damage that's been done in my absence.

I begin in the south-facing front yard. After deadheading what remains of the daffodils and tulips, I carefully rake some of the leaves that remain, just to clean things up a little. Dad always liked to leave a thin layer to nurture the earth. As I kneel, pulling some weeds, Selena Gomez's 'Lose You to Love Me' comes on my playlist. Her words stop me. I stare at the tiny unwanted plant between my fingers. Have I found me? I shake my head. I've only lost you. Tossing the weed in with the other detritus, I tug out my phone to switch to a different playlist. I keep working until the heat of the day forces me into the cooler shade behind the house.

After a quick break to empty my bucket and drink some water, I head to the backyard. While it does need raking, a lot of the plants could really use a pruning. I start by attacking the big rhody back by the fence. When several lower branches are gone, I'm much happier with the shape. Maybe this will encourage it to put out more blooms. As I drag the branches out and begin chopping them into small enough lengths to fit in the yard waste bin, I look up at the maple that lost a limb last January. Has that only been four months? It seems a lifetime ago. Rix did a great job removing the remains. It's nearly healed. Much faster than if I'd done it. He so meticulous about everything. How's he doing? Does he have a safe place to live? I go back to clipping the branches.

By the time the bin's half full, I'm drenched in sweat. My body can't handle the thirty degree leap over only a few days. I drink the last of the water in my bottle and go inside to get some more. Checking my messages, I find one from Rama.

> Hi Maggie. Hope you're having fun in the sun. I'll be off at 3 and wondered if you want to get a bite with me?

He's sweet.

> Sure. I'm not going to want to cook after this. ;-) How about I pick you up? We can eat over here.

> That sounds great. If I don't peter out, maybe we can watch a film.

> Pick you up at 4?

> Perfect. See you then.

It's already two, so I go out to collect my things and put them away. That's enough for one day. After a cool shower, I do my best to shape my hair into soft curls like in that video. I think about leaving it loose, but it's too hot for that. Scrunchie to the rescue.

Rama's waiting outside when I pull into the passenger load zone. He smiles at me while he crawls in and closes the door. "You look lovely."

"Thanks. How was your day?"

"Hectic. I'm tired of this pandemic already, and it's only just begun."

"Isn't that the truth. Is Kwanjai Thai OK?" I scroll through their menu.

"Sure. Get whatever sounds good."

After placing the order, I drive us down Denny toward Seattle Center. "What movie do you want to watch?"

"Have you seen 'Jojo Rabbit?' I hear it's quite well done."

"Oh." I merge onto Highway 99. "I've been meaning to see that."

"Tell me, Maggie, how are you doing?" Rama's voice is gentle and demanding at the same time.

I glance over at him and his pleasant smile. "I'm fine. How are you?"

"Good. Good. But I'm worried you're not getting enough rest. Have you been sleeping well?"

"I dunno. OK, I guess." As we cross the Aurora Bridge, I barely look around at the mountains. "Well, maybe not so good. I keep waking up."

"Why do you think that is?"

When we stop at the light at Fremont Avenue, I put my focus on Rama. "The house is too quiet. Not that Rix was very noisy, but still. It just feels empty." He puts his hand on mine. Why does he stir these things up? I blink away tears. "And *I* feel empty."

The light changes, he removes his hand, and we go pick up our dinner. It's nice to have someone to eat with, and chat with, and just be with. I didn't realize how much I've been missing Rix. The movie's fun, and Rama keeps the conversation light on the trip back to his place.

In my quiet home, Rama's presence lingers, making me feel calm and grounded. I'm blessed to have such a good friend in my life. For the first time all week, sleep— deep and peaceful—does not evade me.

May 11, 2020
Rix

A party begins in the front room when nearly everyone gathers to play online games. With all the chatter and laughter, I can't concentrate. As I stand to leave, Bryer raises her voice over the others. "You should join us. It'll be better with more people."

"I need to work."

A cellphone's blue-white light spills from Corvina's room. After lightly rapping, I nudge the door, which catches on a shoe. Through the narrow opening, I peek inside. Without raising her eyes from the screen, the girl mutters, "Wha'd'ya want?"

"The others are playing games. They need another person. You should join them."

"I like this game."

"So, the phone's working out?"

Her thumbs move in a blur. "Aw, shit." She raises her eyes long enough to say, "It's great. Thanks for gettin' it for me."

"You're welcome." I continue to my room.

The door is closed, so I knock before opening it. Looking up from his book, David smiles. "Hi, Rix."

"I wondered where you were hiding."

"Didn't feel like playing games." He adjusts the pillows behind his back. "I never get any time to myself."

"Oh." I turn to leave. "All right."

"You don't need to go." His voice chases me, bringing me to a stop. "You're so quiet, no one even knows you're in the room." He pats the bed next to him. "Bring a pillow. This has got to be more comfortable than that cot."

When I'm seated beside him, I smile. "Thanks. This is better. What're you reading?"

"A book I got from Corvina." He closes it to expose the cat on the cover. "She said she was done with it."

"How do you like it?" I guess it wasn't a total waste of money.

"It's for kids, but it's actually pretty good." He snugs back into his reading.

As I dive headlong into my second ticket, David scoots closer to watch me work. "What *is* all that?"

"I deploy new code, monitor server systems and fix what goes wrong."

"Wow. How'd you learn to do that?"

"I studied online. It's not like we don't have a lot of free time." Turning my head toward him, my nose brushes the tips of his soft curls, catching the sweet smell of his fruity shampoo. "It's good to find a job where you can work remotely. DevOps pays fairly well."

He drops his head to my shoulder. "I'm not smart enough to do something like that. Couldn't even get accepted at U-dub."

"That doesn't mean a thing. I'm sure you could find something you're good at. The internet has lots of opportunities to learn. How are you paying your rent now?"

"Go back to work." He nestles closer. "I'm just gonna watch for a while."

By the time I track down the issue, David's head lies heavy on my shoulder. Probably asleep, or just needs to be close to someone. He's like most of the vampires I've encountered over the years: late teens or early twenties; not yet educated; not old enough to have been in a strong, loving relationship; never having held their newborn or watched them grow. It reinforces why I'm a loner. His chances of survival are low, and the risk of my losing someone I care about, even just a little, is inversely high. Not to mention the risk he poses to my survival.

Closing my laptop, I slip away, gently lowering his sleep-limp body to the bed, and retreat to my cot. I miss my bed, my room—and Maggie.

May 12, 2020
Rix

Murmured words draw me from my sleep. "Now, I'm a mess," Matt whispers.

"Don't blame it all on me." David's coo is followed by a slurpy smooch.

"I'm gonna clean up."

As Matt leaves, I blink open my eyes. David sits cross-legged on the bed, staring at me with a lascivious grin as he strokes himself. "You're next."

Closing my eyes, I roll away. He moves to sit on the edge of my cot, then runs his fingers through my hair. I look up at him. "Please don't touch me."

"Aw, c'mon, Rix. We've got time. Let's have some fun." His hand returns to his crotch, and his cheeks radiate his excitement in a peachy glow. "Please? I know you slept with

Cleve and Bryer." His hand returns to view, fingers glistening with natural lubricant. "Have you had sex with a vampire? It's so much better. It goes on and on. And, no condoms. No worries about STDs." Bringing his fingers to his lips, he draws each one into his mouth to slowly lick them clean. "I've wanted you to touch me since we first met."

"Look, David"—I turn onto my back and brace myself half-prone on my elbows—"if I was interested in sex, it'd be with someone I love."

He pouts and returns to stroking himself. "I'm *really* good in bed. Matt doesn't appreciate the finer nuances of sexual pleasure. I bet you do."

I keep my eyes locked on his. "I'm not one for casual sex." As the rhythm and intensity of the pumping increases, he lets out a little moan. My gaze dances to his crotch before I can pull it back up to his eyes. "Would you stop that?"

"All right." Standing, he continues to slowly stroke himself. "I wanted to make sure you really don't desire me, and it's not just because of Matt." He flops onto his back on the bed and pumps more vigorously.

I close my eyes and long for the quiet of Maggie's basement.

The door opens. "David," Matt whispers, "why didn't you wait for me?" The bed squeaks under his weight. "Here, baby, let me do that for you."

Rolling to face the wall, I cover my ear with my crooked arm and drift back to sleep to the sound of David's pleasure. The next time I awaken, our room's silent, but the squeaks and bumping of the bed next door are what disturbed my slumber. Doesn't anyone sleep in this house?

Trying halfheartedly to be quiet, I get up and tug on my jeans and t-shirt. My laptop goes under my arm, and I carry my socks and shoes as I tiptoe from the room. The sound of Azul and Erlandr's sex is louder out in the hallway. I creep up the stairs, seeking the solitude of the front room. Corvina is sitting, wedged into a corner at the far end of the farthest couch, tapping away on her phone.

I move into the room. "Do you mind if I sit in here?" Without looking up, she nods. "Oh," I frown, not expecting that. "All right." Her head rises. She blinks, then vigorously shakes her head and returns her focus to her game. "Thanks," I murmur. Settling onto my usual couch, I pull on my socks and shoes—I still haven't gotten used to wearing shoes in the house.

After checking my email and messages, I browse the news. The President continues to downplay the virus, even while members of his staff get sick and twenty thousand new cases are confirmed every day. A new technology using RNA promises to deliver a vaccine in record time. The unemployment rate just hit a post-Depression record of nearly fifteen percent, with almost a quarter of Americans out of work. The Administration's using the pandemic and the worsening economy to justify expansion of immigration restrictions. That's enough news. I dive into my tutorial.

"Shit." Corvina slams the phone down on the cushion, then looks in my direction. "Sorry."

"I'm surprised to see you out here."

"Only when no one else is."

"You should come out more often. Get to know every-one. They don't bite."

"Pfft." She grins. "Is that supposed to be funny?" Her expression grows somber. "They all hate me."

Setting aside my laptop, I move to the other end of her couch. "What makes you say that?"

"Nobody wants me here. Bryer sure doesn't, and Azul —she wants Erlandr all to herself. You're the only one who doesn't hate me."

"Erlandr doesn't hate you. He's just distracted. No one's ever paid attention to him like Azul is." Although, beyond the sex, I don't know what he sees in her. But maybe that's enough. "Matt and David don't hate you. Cleve doesn't. You haven't given them any chance at all to get to know you."

"Yeah, whatever." She thumbs open her phone. "Leave me alone now. I'm about to level up."

3

PROTESTING

May 15, 2020
Rix

Knocking on Azul and Erlandr's door elicits no response. In the front room, I find her—totally focused on her phone—but not him. "Where's Erlandr?"

She looks toward the hallway door. "Try Corvina's room."

As I approach the half-open door, I overhear him, soft voice barely audible over the noise of a video game. "Why don't you come out in the front room?"

Her thumbs move in a blur. "Take that."

"Excuse me." My entry causes Erlandr's head to spin toward me, but Corvina's focus remains locked on her phone. "I'd like to take you hunting again tonight." I raise my voice slightly to be heard over the noise of the game. "That means Corvina needs to come." She ignores me. "Too many of us are hunting at Woodland Park, so we need to go somewhere farther away." Erlandr shrugs. "Corvina," I say, even louder, "did you hear me?"

"I heard you," she snarls, sneering at me. "So take me someplace else."

"I'm thinking of Gas Works. Have you been there?"

Her eyes are back on the phone. "Yeah, yeah." She waves a hand around. "Grassy hills and rusty ol' machinery." She raises her head. "Oh, and the lake. I like the lights on the water."

"I do, too." I'm fishing for something—anything—we might have in common, but she doesn't bite.

"That's nice." She rolls her eyes and looks down at the screen. "When do we go?"

"The sun already set. The nights are so short, we should leave now if we're going to have time for both Erlandr and me to feed."

She stays where she is. "Why do I hafta go?"

"I want you to." I push the rumpled blankets aside to sit on the bed. "Would you look at me, please?" Without moving her head, she glares up at me. "Thank you. I'd like you to watch as I teach Erlandr. To learn more about how not to hurt your victims. There's no point in protesting."

"Oh, all right." She makes a face, but scoots to the edge of the bed. "At least, I'll be outta this room."

"And don't forget your mask."

"I dunno why I hafta wear one. I already died from COVID."

"It keeps us from standing out." I'm tired of having this argument. "Just wear it."

"I still dunno why I had to come." Corvina complains all the way to the park. "It's hard to play Bejeweled, let alone Minecraft." How can she play games and walk, albeit slowly, without tripping, while continuing to talk so incessantly? When we stop to wait for the light at Thirty-fourth, she takes a quick look around. "Aren't we there yet? I'm tired of walkin'." After the light changes, we head across the street. She starts prattling again, "I dunno why we had to come all the way down here." She nearly trips on the curb at the end of the crosswalk. "Shit. Green Lake's so much closer."

"I already explained that it's best to keep moving from place to place."

"Well, I'm glad you didn't make me walk somewhere farther, especially since you're not even gonna let me feed."

I'm happy when we start down the access road on the west side of the park. "Please be quiet now," I say to Corvina, "and put the phone away."

"Shit," she mutters, but slips it into her pocket.

Lowering my voice to barely audible, I add, "Keep a lookout for lone joggers or walkers." I chose this entrance because of the cluster of trees that separates the parking lot from the start of the trail. As we approach the road end, I lead the pair of young vampires onto the grass along the edge of the woods. Listening carefully, I peer into the dark, but don't hear anyone. When I turn to scan the hills, Corvina's gone. "Where'd she go?"

Erlandr thumbs over his shoulder. "Over there. Some boys are throwing a frisbee."

When we're standing beside her, she points to one of the youths. "I want that one."

"We're not here for you tonight. Come on." I nudge her shoulder in the other direction.

"Don't touch me."

"I'm sorry. Please come with us." I lead them to the top of the hill.

Erlandr scans the area around us. The lights of downtown Seattle sparkle on Lake Union, capturing my focus. My favorite view of the city.

Corvina stands beside me, so close her shoulder bumps my upper arm. "It's pretty."

Even though I'm surprised at her comment, I say, "I thought you might like it." Erlandr taps my shoulder and starts down the west side of the hill, a hunter stalking his prey. I follow. "Corvina, come on."

Tearing her eyes from the shimmering city lights, she trudges after me. Halfway down the hillside, a shirtless young man sits in the lotus position, facing the fast fading remnants of the sunset. Erlandr is beside him before he stirs. "Nice spot." He squats right next to the man. "Do you come here a lot?"

Catching Corvina's eye, I hold a finger over my masked lips. She nods. Erlandr's approach impresses me. It seems all he needed was a little coaching. Mask dangling from his ear, he puts his hand on the man's bare shoulder and runs it up to his neck. My phone buzzes, distracting me with news of an unexpected meeting at work.

I glance at Corvina, who licks her lips, and catch a glimpse of her fangs. "Not tonight," I whisper, "and put your mask back on." I understand her reaction. I'm so hungry, it's difficult to remain where I am. Without noticing I moved, I'm two steps nearer. My eyes lock on the man's neck as Erlandr moves his hand away. When his head blocks my view, I move closer. Drool slides down my chin, dampening my mask. When I slip it off to wipe my lips, my hand comes away bloody—scratched by a fang. I lick it.

I'm so close, I touch Erlandr's shoulder. "That's enough." His soft grunting stops. Swallowing, he lifts his head. I restrain myself from pushing him aside. "Cover it with your hand. Think about closing the wound." After rubbing more drool from my lips and looping the mask over my ears, I dig a packet from my pocket, tear it open and hand the wipe to Erlandr. He lifts his hand and wipes away a surprisingly small amount of blood. "Good," I murmur.

When he stands, the man blinks up at him. "That was a great meditation. Join me again sometime." Closing his eyes, he begins breathing deeply.

As Erlandr and I walk up the hill, he asks, "Are you OK?"

"Just hungry. But, I need to get back to attend a meeting. Well done, by the way."

"Thanks." It's barely there, but it's the first time I've seen him smile. After putting on his mask, he looks around. "Where's Corvina?"

"She was just here."

Rushing to the crest of the hill, we spot her lying in the shadows of a recess with the boy she picked out earlier. As she licks his neck, the soft city light glints from her fangs.

"Time to go," I say.

She gives his neck another lick. "Leave uth alone."

"Now, Corvina." I try to be stern without raising my voice above a whisper. "I need to work."

"Oh all right, dad," she hisses, and pulls away from the boy. Flushed and panting hard, he grabs his crotch. "We were just havin' some fun. It's not like I was gonna let him do anything nasty." She stands over him and grins wickedly. Her fangs are gone. "Sorry, but I hafta go."

May 21, 2020
Corvina

Wedged into the corner of my couch, I start up my new Wayward Souls game. I'm not very good yet. I had to beg Rix to install it for me—he's so bossy. Well, it did cost eight bucks, but *still*. No one else is around, so I came out. Maybe Rix or Erlandr will see me. That should make them happy. I don't like being around the others. I focus on my game.

When Rix enters, I glance up. A screech followed by a loud crash brings my attention back to my screen. Shit. I'm never gonna make it to the next level if I can't concentrate.

"Is it all right if I work here?"

I look up as far as his chest. "I don't care." I click restart. "Just be quiet."

David comes in, and I die—again—right as I'm about to get to level three. I scowl at him, but as usual, he ignores me. After dropping to the couch beside Rix, he snuggles against him. "Let's go hunting."

"I'm working." Rix doesn't even look up from his screen.

"You can work later." David nudges the lid. "I'm hungry now."

Me, too.

"What's wrong with Matt?"

"He's mad. He left without me."

Rix runs his hand over his head and gives David a long look. "Just for a little while."

Why don't they ask if I want to go?

When they're on their feet, David puts his arm around Rix and kisses his cheek. He's so gross. "I knew I could count on you." Rix frowns and shrugs him off.

They walk right past me on their way to the door, as if I'm invisible. Footsteps in the stairway make me die again. I don't want to see anyone. I go to my room and continue my game.

"Rix isn't here." Erlandr's voice is so soft, I can barely hear him.

"It's fine." Even though Azul's trying to whisper, her voice is so loud, it comes right through my door. "We'll be back before anyone notices we're gone."

"Let's just wait for Rix."

"Come on," she whines. "I'm hungry, and so few people are out, we shouldn't wait for them all to go to bed. Besides, Bryer and Cleve are here."

"OK." He doesn't sound happy about it.

The front door shuts. Dashing to my door, I open it a crack. From down the hall, I hear bedsprings squeaking, and Bryer and Cleve's grunts. I close the door and pull on my sneakers. It's a short drop from my window to the front walk. I'm free!

To avoid running into Rix or Erlandr, I go to the U-District. Lots of kids hang out over there, and I'm not afraid of the older boys anymore. It's quieter than I expected, but some people hang out by the church on sixteenth. As I stroll past, a blue-haired boy peels away from his group to follow me. He's still there after I go around the end of the building. The parking lot is empty, and all the voices come from the street behind me.

"Hey," he calls. When I stop to look back, he struts up to me. "You new here?"

"First time." I smile. "Just checking things out."

"Nothin' back here"—he slides his arm around my shoulder—"unless you're lookin' for somewhere private."

His eyes running over my body make me feel naked. My stomach clenches, but then, I remember what I am. When I slip my arm around his waist, his back's so hot, it feels like it might blister my skin. "Aren't you a little old for me?"

"If you're old enough to be out here ..." He shrugs and leads me into a dark nook in the wall facing the parking lot. "You're not gonna scream or nothin', are ya?"

"Depends. Are you?" I'm not sure how to do this. He's so tall, I can barely reach his shoulder. How am I supposed to touch his cheek? And what do I do once I reach it?

Lifting me, he braces me against the wall with his body. I avoid his kiss by wrapping my arms around his shoulders. I press my cheek against his pulsing neck. My stomach growls. My fangs come out. I try to press them into his neck, but he wiggles, still trying to kiss me. I grope around, and finally my hand touches his cheek. I wish he'd just stop moving. "Quit your squirmin'." And he does! When I pull my head back to look at him, he gazes back with a stupid grin. Oh, this is too easy.

May 21, 2020
Erlandr

When my phone vibrates, my hand shoots down to cover it. Azul glares at me and sharply whispers, "Erlandr," then returns to following a man who walks alone, carrying his takeout dinner. I pull out the phone.

The text is from Rix.

> Is Corvina with you?

I hurry to catch up with Azul, who follows the man around the corner, disappearing behind the Bartell Drugs. She's on the hunt. Rix will need to wait. By the time I turn the corner, her arm's around the man's shoulders. She leads him into a driveway behind the store. As they near the loading dock, she scans the apartment windows in the next building. After nodding at me, she turns to the man, sandwiching him between her and the wall. I stop at the end of the drive to stand guard and keep a watchful eye on the apartments.

While I wait, I text Rix.

no. with Azul.

We need to find her. I'm heading out. Where are you?

wallingford. in the middle of dinner.

Don't dawdle. Take the U-District. She's familiar with it. I'll check out Green Lake.

kk ttyl

"Psst." When my head jerks toward her, Azul scowls, then waves me over. "What are you doing?" she hisses.

"Sorry." As soon as she lifts her hand, I drop onto the man's neck. I'm nowhere near full when I force myself to stop, but that's the price of hunting in pairs. Pulling away, I put my hand over the wound, like Rix showed me. When he's all tidied up, I walk him out to the street. "What were you doing back there?"

"I don't know." He blinks in confusion.

"Don't forget your food." Azul hands him his bag. "Better get home and eat before it gets cold."

"Right." He takes the bag. "Thanks. There aren't enough kind people in the world."

As soon as he's off, Azul punches my shoulder—hard.

"Ow," I grunt. "That hurt."

"¡Dios mío! Pay attention, or what's the point of going out together?"

"Sorry."

"What was so important you couldn't stand watch for five minutes?"

"Rix texted. Corvina's gone missing. He wants us to go look for her in the U-District."

"We're not done hunting."

"I am," I murmur. "Corvina's my responsibility."

"Oh, all right." Scorn fills her voice. "It's best to split up. But you better find her. I'll beat the living shit out of her."

"You take Forty-fifth."

As I trudge toward Fiftieth, I realize Azul will get there before me. Oh, well. I hope this isn't an indication of what my nights will be like going forward—trying to keep a teenager out of trouble. After crossing Interstate 5, I focus on the sounds that stand out in the mostly quiet streets. At the University Playground, and again at the boarded up Seven Gables Theatre, I stop to listen. Sticking to the numbered streets lets me check out the alleys—good places for privacy.

When I get to The Ave, Azul texts.

> heading south on 15th. after burke museum, i'll check that grassy area on campus.

> kk just got to the ave

Up at the Lutheran Church, folks are finishing free meals, and chatting on the steps or leaning against the building. Walking past, I turn into the alley, then circle around to the north parking lot. No people here. As I move on, a moan stops me. I scan the area. From a recess, I hear Corvina's voice. "Lean down a little more."

When I peek into the alcove, she stares at me with

wide eyes before returning to her meal. I stand guard for a couple minutes before turning back to her. It's hard to watch when I'm still hungry. I nearly push her out of my way to take a share. What would Rix do? I put my hand on her shoulder. "That's enough."

"Uh-uh," she grunts.

"Let him go before you take too much." I give her shoulder a little shake. After raising her head to glare at me, she lets go. "Finish it how we were taught."

She rolls her eyes. "Ya sound just like Rix." She puts her hand over the gash and peers at her victim. "Good boy."

"Did you bring wipes?" I pull out a packet. When she shakes her head, I tear it open and hand her the wet cloth.

As she cleans his neck, she peers at the wound. "It's so cool I can just make it go away." She slithers to the ground.

I take the cloth and hand her a clean one. "Wipe your mouth and hands." Putting my arm around the boy's shoulders, I lead him to the corner of the building. "It was nice meeting you." Without looking back, he heads up the alley. By the time I turn, Corvina's already to the sidewalk. "Hey, wait up."

May 21, 2020
Corvina

"You're not my dad," I scream. "I don't have a dad. Gimme back my phone."

Rix puts it in his pocket. "I pay for this room." How can he keep his voice so calm? He must be mad, too. I'm glad he doesn't punch me, like Buddy did. "I pay for your clothing. I pay for your phone. All I ask is for you to follow a few rules."

"I don't care about your rules." Dropping to the bed, I cover my head with my pillow. "Please don't take my phone," I sob. "Please please please." He sits on my bed—I didn't say he could—and puts his hand on my shoulder, leaving it there til I quit crying. "It's not fair," I moan.

"A lot about us is unfair." Through the pillow, his voice is muffled. "We need to decide how willing we are to be careful." Why won't he just shut up? "If we're not, we not only put ourselves in danger, but everyone who depends on us to be careful." He pats my shoulder. "Turn around and sit up. I'm tired of talking to a pillow." Laying in the darkness is better. "You're not getting your phone back until we talk." He gets up. "Let me know when you're ready. I'll be in the front room."

I spin to sitting. "Don't go." The idea of staying in here without my phone makes my stomach sick. He silently turns. I pat the bed. He sits, but only stares at me. Scooting to lean against the headboard, I cross my legs. "I promise to be good." Did that sound like I meant it?

"You'll never go out alone?" When I nod, his shoulders relax. "Thanks for listening to Erlandr when he found you. I'll take you two hunting in a few days. Let me know when you get hungry again." My eyes drop from his chin to his hand as it reaches into his pocket. He holds out my phone. "I'm trusting you."

"I won't let you down again." As soon as it's in my hand, I power it on. After he goes, I listen to the voices in the next room.

"How'd it go?" Bryer asks.

"I don't know. She seemed sincere," Rix says softly, "but she's fourteen, going on a hundred."

"You should nail the window shut." Azul hates me.

"Don't say that." Erlandr sticks up for me. "She'll be OK."

"I sure hope so," Bryer grumps. "It's bad enough having you lot staying here." I knew it. She hates me, too.

"Could you all be a little nicer?" Rix raises his voice, then brings it back down. "She thinks everyone hates her."

"We don't hate her." That was David. "But it's hard to be nice when all she ever does is snarl at us."

Hiding under my pillow, I start my game. I think I can level up.

May 24, 2020
Maggie

A lthea made me take a day off. Being home when I'm not at work or asleep seems very odd. After sleeping until noon, I sit in my quiet kitchen. The coffee is comforting, the doomscrolling, not so much. The US death toll is at ninety-six thousand. It will likely reach a hundred thousand in the next couple of days.

"I can't believe—" I look up, expecting Rix to be there, but of course, he's not. Everyone I love leaves me. Switching off my phone, I pick up my empty cup and plate, and take them to the sink. I consider adding these to the week of dishes already there. My Dad's words in my head prompt me to mutter, "Keep this pile growing, Maggie May, and you'll break something." I turn on the hot water.

When the dishes are drying, I go up to my room. My list of things to do is so long—laundry; vacuuming; cleaning the bathroom; weeding the yard—I don't know where to begin. The dearth of anything clean to wear other than a pair of shorts and a t-shirt put laundry at the top of the list. To my clothes in the laundry bag, I add my sheets and towels, and head to the laundry room. A lot more hospital clothing waits downstairs.

After starting the first load, I wander down the hallway to see if Rix left anything behind, and how much cleaning I'll need to do before I can look for another renter. In the bathroom, his toilet kit sits on the shelf. Why didn't he take it? That's weird. A tiny bottle of vanilla sits on top. Without touching it, I move on. The towels need washing, of course, but I won't need to spend much time cleaning.

At the bedroom door, I peek around the jamb. Creeping like an intruder, I step inside. I haven't been in here since he left. It feels empty, like something's missing. Aside from a small pile of shirts and socks and things inside the closet—empty hangers all facing the same way —nothing's out of order. He's always so scrupulously tidy. I'll need to wash the sheets, vacuum and dust, and figure out what to do with his things, but it shouldn't take long.

I poke at his laundry with my toe, but resist kicking it. Right on top lies the t-shirt he was wearing the last time I saw him. Tears fill my eyes, unbidden and surprising. I bring the shirt to my face and inhale deeply. How odd. It smells faintly of vanilla. Ohh. No wonder he smells like warm cookies. My shoulders relax. Using the soft, worn fabric, I dry my eyes. After tearing apart the bed, I take the sheets, along with the pile of clothing, to the laundry room. I'll do his towels with mine.

Vacuuming between loads of laundry fills most of the afternoon. I put the dishes away and, just like that, realize I'm hungry. Opening my phone, I text Rama.

> Hungry. Have your plans changed?

> Nope. You should have come in. Amazing Meals for Heroes spread from The Herb Farm! Can't wait! Have you tried Rix?

I take in a sharp breath. Hesitate, not knowing how to reply.

Rama comes to the rescue.

> Sorry. I forgot. I guess not. Have you found a new roommate yet?

> No. Just found some time to clean today. Maybe soon.

> Gotta go. Medic One arriving in 3. May not get that meal after all …

> Stay safe.

I order a pizza, then sit to rest while I wait for it to arrive, mindlessly scrolling through the news. I really need to start ordering healthier meals. Another reason to be at the hospital. The indie playlist plays softly in the background. The CDC says forty percent of transmissions are before people know they're sick, but a third of infections are asymptomatic, so what does that mean? And Dr Fauci—who I truly want to trust—treads on such thin ice between keeping the public as safe as possible and capitulating to the political views of the current administration. How safe is he in his job? Or at home? In one breath, he says we should begin reopening, and in the next, that we should take 'very significant precautions.' It sounds so dire, and yet, so mundane. Is this what we've come to? I wish I had someone to chat with, but we're way too busy at work for small talk. These are the things Rix and I discussed.

As I hum along to the background music, I realize it's the song, "Demons," that I caught Rix singing that day back at the end of last year, when we were still going on coffee dates at Lighthouse. My gut tightens. Could that really only be five months ago? It feels like he's been gone at least that long. What a crazy, mixed up year this has been.

A knock on the door pulls me from my melancholy. Oh, that's right. Pizza. The exchange at the door is COVID quick. The young delivery person seems terrified of me, standing as far away as possible before handing me the box and dashing back to her car. People like her are the totally unsung heroes of this pandemic. The dangers of her job are nearly as great as mine, and even more ignored. And yet, I can't wait to get back to the ER.

May 30, 2020
Rix

I'm so hungry, I barely wait for the sun to set before heading out. The streets are vacant. Even with the national numbers dropping a bit, in Seattle, a slight upturn has folks staying home, worried we may be seeing the beginning of a second wave.

"Caw. Caw. Caw." A crow dives toward me, but pulls up before striking my head. A glittery elastic child's bracelet clacks to the ground at my feet.

"Sorry, my friend." I stoop to retrieve it, then pocket it before looking up. "No scraps tonight."

After circling once, the glossy black bird joins a passing murder. The crows swoop in pairs in intricate dances, darting amongst themselves, joyfully greeting family headed for the evening roost. Their raucous calls fade in the dwindling twilight.

Maybe some joggers will be out for a last-minute run at Green Lake. I arrive to find it nearly empty. Sticking to the shadows in the wooded area along the south end of the lake, I make my way to the old Aqua Theater. Ripples on the surface of the lake reflect the moonlight that makes its way through the gathering clouds, and draw me to the water's edge. A lone jogger runs past, but the shimmering glow enthralls me. I can almost see six tiny flames in six tiny paper boats drifting in the ruffled water. Wresting my eyes away, I listen. No more footfalls. The trail around the lake appears entirely abandoned. I've never been here at this time of day when there weren't dozens of runners, at least. Turning my back on the beguiling water, I continue my hunt.

Murmured voices draw me into Woodland Park. No joggers here—only shadow people, who barely have more rights than me. I smell them before I see them, huddled in the underbrush. The sour smell of weed nearly masks the underlying odor of unwashed bodies and clothing. Far too many unhoused folks are living in the public spaces, with simply nowhere else to go. Skirting the edge of the park, I drop down to Green Lake Way North and make my way toward downtown.

Fremont is deserted. A lone sailboat toots for the bridge to open—a long airhorn blast, followed by a shorter one. The bridge's deeper horn replies with the same pattern. A dinging bell accompanies the gates lowering to block the non-existent traffic, and the bridge deck splits in the center as each side slowly rises. I lean on the rail to watch the boat slip by, nearly silent in the quiet night. I remember sailing with my wife's family and how wonderful it was to glide on the water, with just the wind for power. The bridge deck lowers into place. I trudge on. Maybe I'll find something nearer to Seattle Center.

Dexter Avenue is decidedly too quiet. Since Facebook moved in, people are always out, even during this pandemic. Something's wrong. Sirens wail. My gut clenches. As they near, the pulsating blue lights of a police car rivet my attention. It's not just one, but three, plus a firetruck and an aid car. I find it difficult not to bolt. As they approach Aloha, where I've stopped to wait—like a good Seattleite—for the light to change, I cover my ears as they zoom past. The scintillating lights tug at me to follow. I lose sight of them as they disappear around the corner at Mercer.

A pall of smoke hangs over the city, lit by an angry vermilion glow. Beyond the sirens, the sounds of booms and cries and shattering glass fill the night. The flicker of firelight draws me down Sixth Avenue. I approach a crowd. A crowd! Some of them hold signs. They chant, "I can't breathe." Ah, I remember now. A Black man, George Floyd, was killed by a Minneapolis cop. Except for COVID numbers and the weather, I haven't been keeping track of the news, but this one caught my eye. What kind of person could willfully torture a victim like that—slowly squeezing the life out of him? I shudder.

I didn't realize the rage had cascaded into other cities. I should pay more attention to Twitter, but when I haven't fed for this long, hunger consumes all my thoughts ... well, that and keeping my job, and attending to my newer responsibilities. And, I don't really have anyone where I'm staying who's interested in these things. I miss those morning talks with Maggie. My focus returns to the onlookers.

Since the beginning of the pandemic, I haven't seen so many people in one place. Creeping up behind them, I search for a lone victim to lure away. The flashing lights and flaring fires focus my attention beyond the gathering. A row of black-clad figures—dressed in riot gear, and holding shields and nightsticks and cans of pepper spray—stands between the crowd and what's transpiring further down the street. My anxiety rises, but I can't take my eyes off the unfolding scene.

Illuminated by nearby flames, a bicycle troop of officers arrives at the T-Mobile store. A flurry of opportunists flows from the broken storefront windows, pockets bulging with phones. The smoke from a flash-bang obscures the view. Around me, the crowd grows hushed. Holding its breath. Squinting through the haze. Making out officers pressing several people to the ground, chasing and tackling others. Many protesters break through our line of riot police and run closer to the mayhem.

Through the billowing fog of another flash-bang, a struggle emerges—a squirming young person in an orange hoodie lies face down on the ground while an officer tries to handcuff him. Another policeman joins the first. The crowd around them grows. "Get your knee off his neck!" Those of us still behind the line of police hear it again and again. For just a moment, through the protesters—vying for space, holding up phones, documenting everything—I spot the cause of the chant. The second officer bears his knee down on the neck of the person being arrested. How can this be happening after the way Floyd was murdered? The shouts continue. Taking his eyes from his task, the first officer glances at the agitated throng. He moves his partner's knee to the prone man's shoulder before returning to the handcuffs. They disappear behind the protesters and the smoke. The gawking group around me disperses. Most of the officers bolt down Pine. I go the opposite direction, in search of more privacy.

4

TENUOUS TENDRILS

May 30, 2020
Rix

Approaching an alley, I spot a lone masked person, checking their phone. I glance around. Since no one is nearby, I decide to take a chance. I'm beside them before they look up into my eyes. Slipping my mask from my ear, I let it dangle from the other one. I smile. "Hello."

"Who are you?"

"Put that thing away."

They turn off the phone and shove it into the pocket of their tight pink jeans. With a gentle nudge of my fingertips on their chin, I guide them into the alley. They lean against the wall. When I stroke their cheek, they gasp and turn their head away to expose their neck, cleanly shaven beneath the makeup. I dislike the taste of makeup and might normally use a little spit to wash some away, but tonight—hungry and rushed—I don't bother. My fangs extend. I open my mouth.

Boom! A bright flare. Too bright. Noxious gas drifts toward us. My eyes burn. Turning my head away, I squeeze them shut. My victim coughs and gags. I let them go. As they dash away, I follow. At the far end of the alley, we emerge onto Pike. The air clears. I blink and squint. Someone rushes up to me with a bottle of water and, before I can speak, pours it over my face. My victim is assaulted in a similar manner.

"I'm fine," I sputter.

"Did any get in your eyes?"

Fluttering butterflies take flight in my belly. "Maggie?"

She takes a step back. "What are you doing here?" Her shocked face softens and glows a muted amber. Good. She's not afraid of me. "And where's your mask?" She dangles one on the end of her finger.

"I lost it"—I wave my hand toward the alley—"somewhere back there." My hunger tugs at me. Hooking the mask behind my ears, I steal a glance at my intended victim, but my eyes return to Maggie. "Are you safe?"

"For now, but a curfew's in effect, so we're not really supposed to be out here. And neither are you. Didn't you get the alert on your phone?"

I totally ignored that. "Maybe you shouldn't be doing this. It's dangerous."

"We're fine. We keep moving." She's not convincing. "Look at these people. They need us." My eyes follow the sweep of her hand.

"Just be careful. It was nice bumping into you."

When I begin to turn, her hand lands on my arm.

"Stay?" Her dark eyes sparkle. "Please? We're short-handed. Rama took an extra ER shift because of this. Even if you just hand out masks, we can use the help." She uses her forearm to push her hair from her face. "I don't know what to do with this hair. My mother used to braid it, but she never taught me how." The corners of her eyes pinch in pain, then it's gone. "Now, this drizzle's turning it all frizzy. I lost the band hours ago. It'd be easier to just cut it off."

"Don't do that. Hold on." From my pocket, I fish out the child's bracelet the crow gave me. "I have something that may work." I wrap the elastic around her dark, thick curls. In the pale light of the single streetlamp, the plastic jewels shimmer along with the mist that clings to her hair. "How's that?"

"Thanks." She's already distracted by another hacking protester. "Come help me." My intended victim walking away captures my attention. I find it difficult to pull my eyes from them when Maggie calls, "Rix, what are you doing?"

"Are you sure they're OK to walk home alone?" Yanking my focus away, I put it on Maggie. "I could go with them, then come back to find you."

"I need you here, now." She shakes her head adamantly. "Besides, you'll never find us again. They'll have to make it on their own."

"What do you need?"

We grab everything, and move four times over the next couple of hours. As the streets become more chaotic, we end up further and further from downtown. I nudge us northward, ending up near Seattle Center. Around eleven-thirty, we use the last of the water and milk. The pull carts are nearly empty, with no more masks and very little medical supplies left.

Maggie calls someone to bring more, but this time nothing remains to restock us. "Well, that's that." She turns to the others—who I never got a chance to meet. "We can go home now. Can you take the wheelies up to Althea's? It's just as close for me to get home from here as to go there and catch a ride with one of you."

"No worries," the woman says. "See you next time." The group heads up Denny Way toward the Hill.

The light by the Pink Elephant Carwash brings us to a halt. I ask, "How're you getting home? The buses aren't running."

"I quit riding the bus. I don't want to catch COVID. I'll walk. It'll give me a chance to unwind." Turning her head, she scans the intersection. "So much has changed here, I hardly recognize the city anymore. I guess the Pink Elephant's next to go."

"It's inevitable."

When the light changes, she starts to cross. I hesitate —thinking about resuming my hunt—but when the walk signal begins flashing red, I trot after her. "I'm going the same way. Do you mind if I walk with you to Fremont?"

"All right." That was halfhearted, but maybe because she's tired?

After cutting over to Dexter, we silently walk to the light at Aloha. "If we cut down to the lake from here"—my voice booms in the quiet night—"we can walk along West-lake. No hill."

She contemplates me. What's going on behind those

eyes? "All right." The streets are devoid of people. When Maggie removes her mask, I do as well. She breathes in deeply. "That feels good." At the lakeside trail, we join a number of others heading north, most likely walking home from the protest. Maggie's stride becomes freer. "I've never walked down here."

Her voice surprises me, causing my head to swivel toward her with a snap. "It's a nicer walk than Dexter." Noticing Maggie is again wearing her mask, I don mine.

"I didn't know Facebook expanded down this far. Soon, they'll own the entire west side of Lake Union."

"Probably."

She doesn't speak again until we approach the Aurora Bridge, where she stops to tug down her mask and gaze at a small community of houseboats. "They're so pretty. I sometimes think it'd be easier to maintain a houseboat than a yard."

"Didn't they film 'Sleepless in Seattle' down here?"

For the first time all night, she smiles. "That sounds right." She starts walking again. "We should keep going."

"It's been a long night. You're not working tomorrow, are you?"

"I wasn't planning to, but tomorrow night another protest is likely." She takes a deep breath, lets it out through her lips, making them flutter, then pulls up her mask. "Like we needed this in the Age of COVID-19."

"Don't blame the protesters. Civil unrest peaks in times of crisis."

"Oh, I don't blame them, just the situation that makes protesting necessary."

We stop to wait for the light at Thirty-fifth and

Fremont. I risk brushing my fingertips down her arm. "May I walk you all the way home?" As she silently studies me, tightness grabs my chest, drawing my shoulders inward. I hope that didn't sever this tiny connection. "Please, I'd like to pick up some of my things." I grimace behind my mask. "Unless you've thrown it all out."

"I haven't touched anything— Well, I did do your laundry." The light changes. A rosy warmth kisses her cheeks. "You can walk me home. How've you been?"

I shrug, which relaxes my shoulders as much as her words. "As good as can be expected during a pandemic. Are you still working too much?"

"Yeah, but they need me." She glances at me. "The house is too quiet, anyway, since ..."

"I miss you, too."

As we wait for the light at North Thirty-ninth, the mist condenses into tiny droplets. I peer at Maggie. "Are you warm enough?"

"After the past couple of days being eighty, I didn't dress for this cool drizzle."

"You can wear my hoodie." I start to unzip it.

She regards me with an indecipherable expression, shakes her head—"I'm fine"—and focuses on the cross signal. "Thanks anyway." When the light changes, she steps off the curb and continues toward home.

Once we turn up Phinney Avenue North, we take off our masks, but the steepness of the hill precludes any more conversation from her. When we arrive, she trudges up the porch steps. Over her shoulder, she says, "Wait there." She unlocks the door and goes inside, then comes down and hands me a key. "Go ahead and keep it until you've gotten all your things." She immediately heads back up. I stare at the little metal show of trust in my open palm. At the top, she faces me. "Thanks for all your help tonight. I really appreciate it."

"Sleep well, Maggie May." It comes out as a whisper.

Her tired smile is barely there, but her cheeks hold a faint amber radiance. "Goodnight, Rix."

June 2, 2020
Rix

Soft grunting pulls me from my sleep. "Shh," David whispers. "You'll wake him."

"Screw him," Matt mutters between pants.

David giggles. "I don't think he's into boys."

"It's all right." I roll to sitting—keeping my eyes diverted—and pull on my clothing. "I'm up. I'll leave you to your pleasure." Grabbing my laptop, I go out to the front room where Bryer's sitting on the couch.

"Did the boys bother you?" She smirks. "I can hear them all the way out here."

"At least, I'm not sharing a bed with them." I smile. "Like I did with Robert."

"That must have been unpleasant."

I nod wearily. Rubbing my forehead, I try to push away the drowsiness. After logging onto my computer, I open the Signal app Maggie began using for added privacy at the start of the protests. It's a good idea. I have everyone in the house using it now. Even though no new texts await

me, she's been quickly responding to mine and occasion-
ally initiating conversations.

> Hi Maggie.

I send the text, then browse the latest news.

The city-wide curfew due to the protests has not kept
protesters away. Last night, up on the Hill near the East
Precinct, for the first time in that neighborhood, the cops
used flash-bangs and tear gas, turning the until then
peaceful protest into a riot ... well, they actually declared
it a riot, then made it into one. This is not a new tactic.
Don't they care about the folks whose businesses and
homes filled with the toxic chemicals from weapons that
were banned by The Geneva Protocol of 1925? Weapons
that target the *lungs* during a pandemic rooted in deadly
pneumonia? Things never change. One good thing to
come out of the protests is that the plethora of people on
the streets since Saturday has kept my belly filled. I
hunted successfully on both nights.

Maggie's text seizes my attention. With each digital
exchange, her tenuous tendrils reaching out give me hope
for repairing the damage I've done to our friendship.

> Hi. What's up?

> Just checking in to make sure you're OK.
> Did you go out last night? To the
> protests?

> Yes. Going again tonight. You should
> join us.

I need to work.

Damn. I'd sure like to take the opportunity to reconcile some more with her.

Writing to ask if it's OK to pick up more things.

Sure. Whenever. Before I can reply, another text arrives. Can you come out with us for a few hours tonight? Anything would help.

What time?

Things don't heat up until after dark. Setting up at 9:30.

I'll retrieve my things some other night.

OK. Where do we meet?

NW corner of Cal Anderson. Close to East Precinct.

On foot. Can't be there til 10:30. Is that too late?

Heading over at 9. Pick you up?

This is an unexpected development.

Corner of 50th & Woodland Park. Across from the parking lot. Ten after?

> Sounds good. SYL

A text from Nalini pops up. At four-thirty? She's up early.

> Good news. Your contract renewal was approved.

> Thanks for letting me know! BTW
> Working early today.

> KK TTFN

Plenty of tickets vie for my attention. As I close my fourth one, I check the time—already eight-forty—and call it a day.

At nine, I'm waiting beside the door. At nine oh one, I dash the three blocks to the rendezvous point. As I wait, two crows dive-bomb my head, cawing and scolding. "Hey. It's just me." They flap higher and dance over my head before retreating to their nest in a tree on the other side of the street. A car flashes its lights, then swings to the curb to stop. I climb in.

Maggie smiles. "I'm glad you could come."

As we drive through the U-District, Maggie talks on her phone. "Hi, Althea. On my way. I got the water. Do we need anything else?" She wears earbuds, so I don't hear the response. "Oh. I'm bringing a friend. Yeah, he's got some medical training. OK. See you soon."

To the hum of the steel grating on the University Bridge, I watch two single-person sculls oar past on the canal, bathed in the last golden glimmer of the sunset.

"Pretty, isn't it?" Maggie's voice causes my head to swivel. Her face glows in the same soft light—or maybe it's just her.

"Not as beautiful as you." I look out the window and shrink into my seat. How does she always do this to me? "I'm sorry. I didn't mean to say that aloud."

"You're as charming as ever," she giggles. When I take a peek at her, she glances over and smiles before returning her eyes to the cars around us. "I kinda miss that." This woman is confounding. A red light gives her a moment to put her entire focus on me. "I've been thinking."

"About what?"

"You."

"What about me?"

"Maybe, instead of taking your stuff out"—when the light changes, her head pivots back to the road—"you should move back in."

"I don't understand. Aren't you afraid of me? For that matter, what am I doing in your car tonight?"

"I freaked when you told me." She glances my way. "How was I supposed to react?"

"That's why I didn't tell you."

"I understand that now. But tell me this"—she takes her eyes off the road, landing them on me—"and you need to tell the truth." Returning her focus to her driving, she sucks on her lower lip. "Have you enchanted me? Have you ever bitten me, and I just don't remember?"

"No, Maggie," I sputter—too loud. "I would never do that. Not to you."

She pulls the car into a driveway and turns it off, then

twists in her seat to face me. "You promise you're telling the truth?"

"I swear. I would *never* hurt you. I protect you."

Her brow creases. "From what?"

"Other vampires," I murmur. "I told them not to touch you."

Her eyes grow large. "Other vampires?"

I shrug. "Do you think I'm sui generis?"

"I never thought about that." She studies me intently.

"So, you're OK with me moving back in?"

"As long as you don't have any of your friends over."

"I wouldn't call them my friends. More like ... associates. I've been really careful not to let anyone know where you live." I tear my eyes from her to study my hands. "I don't have friends." How did that slip out? My fingers jitterbug on my thighs.

"You have me." She puts her hand on mine, so gently I don't jerk it away. The dancing stops. "I'm your friend."

My eyes fill. I roughly wipe them with my sleeve, but tears escape. Turning my head away, I rest my forehead in my hand. Maggie still clutches the other one. "Thanks," I croak, and finally look up at her. "You're full of surprises."

"I'm not the only one. We better get going." After handing me a tissue, she reaches for the door. "Don't want to be late for the riot."

June 2 to 3, 2020
Rix

After a hectic, but relatively uneventful night of tending to protesters, Maggie returns me to where she picked me up, pulling into the gated drive that leads to the parking lot at Woodland Park. The horizon already carries a faint pink blush.

"Thanks for the ride." In the amber glow of the street-lamp, I longingly take her in—her face, her hair, her cheeks, her lips. And those mysterious black orbs. I never want to look away.

"Thanks for coming tonight." A smile warms her tired eyes. "I really appreciated you being there."

"You're welcome."

"When'll you come home?"

"I haven't had time to decide. I have responsibilities that I need to sort out." I shrug. "Maybe Friday night. Will that work for you?"

She nods. "I'm working late, but I'm taking Saturday off. I need a rest."

"That'll be good for you." I gaze at her for far too long, but she just peers back. "I'm so happy to be moving back in. I missed you."

"Me, too." She stifles a yawn. "We should both go get some sleep."

Wrenching my eyes away, I fumble with the seatbelt. When I open the door, we both blink in the sudden brightness. "Goodnight, Maggie May."

"Goodnight, Rix."

I watch her car until it disappears on the other side of

the 99 overpass before heading to the house. When I'm inside, Bryer glances up from the couch. "You're out late."

"I went to a protest. With Maggie."

"What?" She moves as if to rise, but Cleve's hand on her arm stops her. "She's seeing you again?"

"Mm-hm."

"How's that work?"

"I don't know yet." I sit on the nearest couch. "I was as surprised as you. She asked me to move back in."

"What about Corvina?" Cleve asks.

"Yeah," Bryer nearly shouts. Cleve's hand slides down to hers, tempering her anger and the volume of her voice. "What about Corvina?"

"I'm sure we can figure something out."

Bryer shakes her head and snorts. "Jeez, Rix. I don't know why I took you in. You bring *children* into my house. And then, you just walk away."

"I really can't keep my eyes open." Standing, I sheepishly ask, "Is it all right to wait until this afternoon to talk about it?" That'll give her some time to cool off.

"Pfft." She waves her hand dismissively. "Just. Go."

After dozing restlessly for several hours, I head up to see if Corvina's awake. She's in the front room, head buried in her phone. Sitting in the middle of her couch, I wait.

"Wha'd'ya want?" she mutters without looking up.

"I need to talk to you."

"So talk." The lights from her game dance on her face.

"I need your full attention."

"Hold on." She taps frantically, then breaks into a grin. "Did it!" She looks up, cheeks radiant with her victory.

"Congratulations."

She sets the phone aside. "Wha'd'ya need?" she asks in the friendliest voice I've heard from her.

"Um." I hate to spoil her mood. "I want to know how you'd feel if I moved out." The words tumble out way too fast. Her cheeks glow a fiery vermilion. She just sits there, seething, looking like she might cry. I hold my palms up. "I'll be close by," I offer weakly. "You can text whenever you need me."

Springing to her feet, she turns to glare at me. The glow of her cheeks turns to flames. "I don't need you."

"Corvina." I stand. "It'll be better. This house is too crowded."

"You hate me," she roars, "just like everyone else."

"Keep your voice down. The others are still sleeping."

Behind her, Bryer appears, blinking her sleep away. "What's all the ruckus? Oh." She looks between me and the girl. "You told her."

Corvina spins toward her. When she scoots behind me and peers around my shoulder, I mutter, "How'd you guess?"

"Can I go to my room?" Corvina sounds small and vulnerable.

I look over my shoulder. "I'd prefer if you stay a bit longer. I'd like to talk some more."

"Oh, all right." She plops down on her couch and opens her phone. For all her sullenness, I'm glad she's back to her normal self.

I return to where I was sitting. Bryer sits close to us, on the next couch over. "If he's moving out, you'll have me to answer to." I shake my head slightly, but she continues. "And I'm not nearly as tolerant as he is. It starts now. Put the phone down." Corvina surprises me by turning it off and slipping it into her pocket. Bryer smiles and nods. "Good. So first off, Rix will come by in the evenings." She meets my eyes. "Right?"

"Um." That wasn't in my plans. "Yes. I'll come by in the evenings."

"Good. You're both listening. Next, you come to me when you need anything: someone to hunt with; a new shirt; someone to cut your hair"—her voice softens—"someone to help with your makeup." This elicits a slight smile from the girl. Bryer firms her voice. "You'll keep your room neat, your clothing, your bedding and your body washed. I don't want to smell you. Got it?" She waits for a nod. "You come out and sit with our family. You're part of it. You need to have your say. And we need to get to know you." When Corvina glances at me, Bryer growls, "Don't look to him to bail you out. Besides, it's what he's been asking since you arrived."

"OK."

"This is only a trial. If you mess up, he's moving back in. And he probably won't like that." She turns her focus on me. "Especially since he'll be sharing your room."

June 5 to 6, 2020

Rix

Late Friday afternoon, I do my laundry. While I fold and pack it, David watches from the bed. "Don't be a stranger, OK?"

Looking up, I smile. "Bryer won't let me off that easily. I'll be here in the evenings."

"Oh." His face brightens to a rosy glow. "Good. I'll be sure to hang out til you come by."

I stop my folding. "Can you keep an eye on Corvina? Maybe ask her to go out to hunt? She gets hungry, too."

He scrunches up his nose. "She's so mean to me."

"Please? Try to interact with her? She's really lonely." I fold the cuff of a sock over its mate. "I'm so old, I'm entirely out of my element with her."

"You're not that old." He giggles, then grows serious. "Are you? How old are you?"

"Older than the Viaduct." I keep my face deadpan as he creases his brow in thought. "It first opened in 1953." Should I share more than that?

"Seventy years ago?" he whispers. "How much older?"

"I'm a hundred and ten."

"Oh my god! You *are* old."

"So, you can see my dilemma."

He flops to his back. "Oh, all right." He sounds as young as Corvina.

"David." I wait for him to lift his head. "How old are you?"

"Nineteen."

"Before? Or total?"

"Total." He shrugs. "A little over a year ago, after doing poorly on my SAT, my dad caught me with another boy—you know—and he threw me out."

"I'm sorry." I say it even though I know how useless it is.

"I don't think he meant for it to be permanent, but he's got a temper. Did you get along with your dad?"

"I was pretty young when he died." I stuff a pair of socks down the side of the pack. "During the previous pandemic."

David's eyes grow wide. "There was another pandemic?"

"The Spanish Flu. Just over a hundred years ago. He was in Europe, fighting the Germans."

"I thought that was in the Forties."

"That was the Second World War. The one I fought"—my shoulders sag—"and died in."

His frown is surrounded by a soft sage blush—his grief for me. "Oh." In typical David fashion, the sadness dissipates as quickly as it arose. Spinning to sit facing me, his face shines with bright yellow anticipation. He grins. "Tell me about your girl."

"Well, she's a woman, not a girl. A strong woman. A nurse practitioner. She's kind and compassionate."

"Is she beautiful?"

I stop packing. Is she? "She has the most amazing eyes."

"Sounds nice. I hope it works out."

"Me, too."

After I finish, I sling my pack over my shoulders, grab Corvina's clean clothes and sheets, and head upstairs.

Dropping my pack by the door, I go into her room—as tidy as I've seen it—to make her bed.

She follows me in. "Thanks for washin' my stuff. Can ya show me how next time?"

"Sure." At the head of the bed, I unfurl the bottom sheet and toss part of it to the foot. "Grab that and you can give me a hand making this up." She rolls her eyes, but takes a pocket and slides it over the corner. When the bed is made, we sit quietly, side-by-side, each pulling on a pillow case. I remember sitting beside my mother, doing the same. "Many hands make light work," I murmur.

"I guess." She crinkles her nose and peers sidelong at me. "You say the weirdest things."

As the sun sets, I shoulder my pack. Everyone else is in the front room.

"You're still here?" Azul sarcastically gibes.

"Don't worry," David says. "He's leaving."

Silently slipping up behind me, Corvina grasps my hand. I look at her, try to smile. She won't meet my eyes.

"Don't forget your promise," Bryer says sternly. "I expect you back here at nine-thirty tomorrow night."

"I'll be here." Shaking my hand free from Corvina's, I check the time. "I guess this is it. Good hunting."

I close the door to a chorus of "good hunting."

Maggie's house is dark when I arrive. She won't be home until after midnight. It feels strange to let myself into her basement. Can it only be a month since I left? My room looks the same. A small stack of the clothing I left behind sits clean and folded on the corner of the bed. On the dresser lies eight hundred-dollar bills—my rent money for May. Shaking my head, I unzip my bag, unpack and stow everything. I take a nice, long, hot shower. My little bottle of vanilla still sits on top of my toilet kit. I remove the cap and inhale, then daub a tiny bit on my neck. The sweet aroma always relaxes me, probably because it reminds me of baking cookies with my daughter. By the time I settle onto my bed to check my email, feet clomp up the front steps. The door shuts.

Maggie?

I send the text, and return to my mail.

Footsteps on the floor upstairs. Shuffling and bumps. The scuff of slippered feet fading up the stairs. Water running. A message alert ping.

Oh, hi. Are you home now?

Not home.

I'm here.

Are you decent?

That's a matter of opinion, but I'm dressed, if that's what you mean. ;-)

BRT

I put my computer away and switch on another lamp. Even though I left the door open, Maggie knocks as she pokes her head around the doorjamb. "Hi."

"Hi. Come on in." I pat the bed next to me.

After a quick glance at the chair, she sits facing me on the bed. "How're you?"

"Good. Better, now." I smile. "How was your night?"

"Just glad to be home." Her finger follows a line in the subtle paisley design of the blanket. She looks up. "I'm glad you're here. I missed you." I can only nod, not remembering how to breathe while caught in the gaze of her dark eyes. She pats my knee. "You must be tired. I know I am. How 'bout we talk in the morning?"

I get up with her, breathe her in. "Sleep well, Maggie May."

June 6, 2020
Maggie

After sleeping late, way past my usual wakeup time, I get up and stretch. I'm still tired, but not as exhausted as I usually am. The long, hot shower feels good and wakes me up even more. I take my time with my hair. Everyone says how lucky I am to have such thick curly hair, but they don't know the half of taking care of it. Maybe I should cut it short—I understand now why Dad liked it that way—but Rix asked me not to. The extra care turns the mess into soft, bouncy curls. I wish it always looked like this. I head downstairs and start the coffee, then text Rix.

> Are you awake? Sorry it's so late.

I retrieve half a bagel from the freezer and pop it into the toaster. My phone vibrates.

> I'm up. How're you this morning?

> Good. Join me for coffee?

> BRT

While waiting for the bagel to brown, I nibble on a banana. The coffee brewing is so loud, it nearly drowns the knock on the basement door.

"It's unlocked," I call. "Come on in." Rix peers shyly from the doorway. "The coffee's nearly ready. Have a seat," I mumble around a mouthful of banana. "I don't bite." I giggle at my little joke, but Rix's smile is forced. He slides onto a stool. The toaster pops. After snatching the bagel, I quickly drop it onto a plate and smear it with butter, then fill two cups with coffee and join Rix at the island. "Done." I smile at him.

The bright daylight makes the cool ashiness of his olive skin really noticeable, but his brown eyes are warm and dreamy, even though he squints. The pupils seem far too large, as if dilated for an eye exam. He takes his time moving his gaze from me to his cup, and takes a sip. "Mmm. I love your coffee." This time, his smile is real. His eyes come back to me. "I like what you've done with your hair."

He noticed! Heat rushes to my cheeks. I hope I'm not visibly flushed. "Thank you."

"What have you been up to?"

"Lots of work." Taking a bite of my bagel, I chew

slowly. He waits for me to continue. "It's just been too lonely here"—I examine a rough edge on my thumbnail, then return my focus to him—"with you gone."

"It was hard for me, too." He sips his coffee. "How's Rama? I still haven't met him."

"He's good. He's always good. Upbeat. You'll like him." I lift my cup, then set it down. "We should have him over for din—" I brush some crumbs into my napkin. "Um ... for a movie. Or to play games."

When I bring my eyes up, Rix smiles and nods. "That'd be fun."

"It's still weird, knowing what I know, but it helps me make sense of you."

"I'm sorry I didn't tell you sooner, but you're the first breathing person I've trusted with this." He focuses on his hands. His voice becomes hushed. "It probably would've made things easier." Looking up, he grins. "You would've thrown me out earlier." His smile fades. He whispers, "And I wouldn't have had the chance to fall in love with you." His eyes drop to his cup.

My cheeks are on fire. I don't know how to respond to that admission. I reach across to gently put my hand on his—still surprisingly cool. He doesn't pull away, but looks up at me. I meet his eyes. "Maybe. But maybe I would've just let you stay. I don't know. I felt deceived, and that made me angry."

"I'll try not to hide things from you again."

End of Volume Three: Vampire House

VOLUME FOUR: VAMPIRE ROUNDUP

1

SPARRING

June 11, 2020
Rix

Being back at Maggie's is disconcerting. It's so quiet. I feel like an intruder in my old room. How long until I start to feel comfortable here again? My phone vibrates with a text from Maggie.

> Good morning, Rix. Breakfast?

She must be as nervous as I am. Another text quickly follows.

> I mean, coffee?

> Sure. BRT.

Some of my tension leaves. I find the return to this little ritual very soothing.

As I slide onto my usual stool, with a steaming cup of coffee already awaiting me, Maggie sets a plate holding a toasty almond croissant onto the countertop and sits on the other side. Gazing at me, she sips her coffee. "Tell me what's going on in the world. I never find time to keep up."

"Well." I drink a few swallows while I think. "The President chastised Inslee and Durkin about the occupation up by the East Precinct. I guess some people are now calling it CHAZ for Capitol Hill Autonomous Zone, instead of CHOP." I take another sip. "The President tweeted, and I quote, 'Take back your city now. If you don't do it, I will. This is not a game.' I can't imagine the military would agree to that. It seems like a bluff to me."

"He likes to bluster, that's for sure. But it is worrisome." She licks the frost of powdered sugar from her lips, takes another bite. "I wonder how the Governor, or the Mayor, will respond."

I smile. "Mayor Durkan already tweeted back."

With a big grin, Maggie leans closer, conspiratorially. "What did she write?"

"'Make us all safe. Go back to your bunker.'"

She mocks a gasp. "Good for her."

"I'm sure Inslee will respond, but probably a little more politically correct, since he's up for re-election."

"The news is fun when you tell it." She finishes her coffee and gets up to put her plate in the sink. "Another cup?"

Despite the coffee, I sleep well during the day. Maybe I'm getting used to the quiet again. Even so, I wake up groggy. The chaos of Bryer's house kept me from sound sleep. I do so much better on my own. When the sun begins to set, I reluctantly pack up my things to head over there.

For once, the front room is silent. As soon as I settle onto the couch and open my laptop, Corvina storms through, like a sudden squall on a dead calm tropical sea. "Why's everyone so mean to me?" She scowls at me and continues to her room. The house returns to quiet.

I debate going to ask her what's wrong, but four texts await me. Balancing work with this community is a challenge. David saunters in and plops onto the couch beside me. I give him a sidelong glance. "I'm trying to work."

"I just came to say hi. You don't have to snarl at me, too." He crosses his arms and pouts.

Setting my laptop aside, I put my entire focus on him. "Hi." I wait for him to meet my gaze. "What did you say to Corvina to make her so upset?"

"Nothing." His face burns in shades of saffron with his lie.

"Who did?"

He huffs—an impressive display of breath control, for a vampire. "I donated that cat warriors book she gave me to the library when I finished it. Like I do with *all* my read books."

"It was a gift from me to her."

"How was I supposed to know that," he snaps, "or that she'd want it back?"

"Well"—I turn sideways on the couch, drawing up my knee—"you can't unscramble eggs."

David stifles a smirk. "I've never heard that one before." He giggles, back to his usual cheerful demeanor. "But I understand what you're saying. I suppose I should go apologize."

"Why don't you invite her to hunt with you? It would be a good opportunity to make amends."

June 11, 2020
David

I can't believe I let Rix talk me into hunting with Corvina. She's such a baby about everything. "I don't wanna go all the way to Gas Works." "Do I hafta?" "Why do I hafta go with David?" She really doesn't like me. Does she think *I* want to spend time with a fourteen-year-old? I wouldn't mind going out with Rix—but he never asks. Besides, he usually gets to hunt alone. He doesn't have to follow Bryer's rules. Well, he does work a lot and pays for three shares in the house. I wonder if he can afford to pay for me, too.

"This is so far." There she goes again.

"You think this was my idea?" I can't keep the disdain from my voice. She punches me. "Ow," I yelp. "That hurt."

"Sorry." She actually sounds sincere. "I sometimes forget to hold back."

"Me, too. I shouldn't have said that." Rix is right. She *is* just a girl.

She's quiet for the final blocks leading to the park. When I head for the main entrance, she tugs my sleeve. "Rix takes us in over here." She leads me to a side road. Sure enough, it goes in a back way.

"Cool," I say in a friendlier voice. "I didn't know about this."

"Shh," she whispers. "Pay attention. Ya might learn somethin'." I roll my eyes, but her focus is on the woods to our left. Peering into the trees, I don't see anyone. She must not, either. She turns up into the hills. "This way."

Skirting the edge of the ridge line, we scan the slopes for people out alone. I spot a guy, sitting in the lee of the hill, gazing at the city lights, but Corvina's already moving toward him. When we're a couple of yards away, she puts her palm on my chest. "Stand guard." She seems to know all the rules. I don't argue because I don't want to ruin the opportunity, but I'm hungry, too. Matt always lets me go first. She walks up to the man and squats next to him before he notices her. "Pretty, isn't it?"

"Yeah." His chin tugs down on his mask. He must have forgotten to close his mouth after the word.

She puts her hand on his neck. "Would ya stand for me?" When he's on his feet, she moves higher up the slope, putting her eye-to-eye with him. "Just think happy thoughts." She tugs off her mask and dives right in.

I salivate, then remember to keep watch. It's hard. My gaze keeps drifting back to her and the man. Moving closer, I stare. "When's it my turn?"

Pulling her mouth away, she quickly replaces it with her hand. She licks most of the blood from her lips, careful not to catch her tongue on her receding fangs. I can't wait any longer and nudge her away. She lets go, replaces her mask and wanders up the hill a ways, constantly peering around. It seems I just got started when her hand lands on my shoulder. "Stop," she says softly.

I lift off to say, "Thtill hungry."

Shrugging, she holds out a hand wipe. When I reach for it, she smacks me. "What're ya doin'? Ya gotta stop the bleedin' first." She covers the wound with her hand. "Don't ya know anything?"

"Matt does all this stuff." I say, indignantly.

"Oh. Well, put your hand here." Her eyes crinkle with a grin. "It's pretty cool." When she lifts her hand, I replace it with mine. All I notice is the vein throbbing. And how hungry I still am. "Think about stoppin' the bleedin'." She puts her hand over mine, and presses down a little. My palm begins to tingle. "Feel anything?" When I nod, she moves away and goes back to peering around.

"How long do I do this?"

"Just be patient."

I've never stayed with a victim like this. Must be what takes Matt so long. I always thought he was just taking more than his share.

She comes back. "Pull your hand away a little." Poking her head in close, she peeks under my palm. "That's good. Take a look." It stopped bleeding! She hands me a wipe. "*Now* clean it off. And be sure to git it all."

We leave the man back where he was, gazing at the lake, and head to the top of the hill to look for our next victim.

"Thanks for teaching me that." I smile at her. I hope she can tell behind my mask. "It is cool."

"Haven't ya ever hunted alone before?"

"Matt found me right after it happened. Man, was I wild."

"Erlandr"—her brow furrows—"was with me. And then, Rix found us."

"I like Rix. I wish he still stayed at the house."

She looks very sad. "Me, too."

"I'm sorry I gave your book away." I rub a drop of blood from the back of my hand, then look up at her. "I didn't know it was a gift."

Studying me, she must decide I'm being sincere. Her eyes smile. "I guess someone else can read it now. You're not so bad, after all. Thanks for huntin' with me."

June 15, 2020
Rix

When I arrive at the house, just after dark, Bryer is waiting with Matt in the front room. "Good. You're here."

"Hi, Bryer." I nod at the young man. "Matt."

"Hey," he grunts. His face holds a fiery glimmer. Is he mad at me?

Turning to Bryer, I ask, "What's up?"

"Matt's going out with you tonight."

That will cut into my work time, but I don't think I'd win an argument with Bryer right now. "All right." I glance at him, but he's staring at the floor. From the hallway, Corvina peeks out. I give her a little smile. She waves, her face a swirl of conflicting emotions—anger, jealousy, affection—muddy and muted. I should take her hunting soon. Putting my attention back on Bryer, I ask, "Any particular reason? Not that I mind."

"It's come to my attention that Matt doesn't know how to share information. I thought maybe you could teach him how to teach others, since you seem fairly good at it."

"OK. I can't stay out too late. I need to work."

"Get moving, then."

For the first block, Matt walks a few steps behind me. When we stop to cross Fiftieth, I turn to him. "What's going on with you and Bryer?"

"Nothing." He steps off the curb. "Let's just hunt."

As we enter the park, I catch up and walk beside him. The dry weather brought out some late evening joggers. We isolate our first victim before even getting to the dog park. I let Matt go first, standing guard until it's my turn. When I clean the woman up and send her on her way, I can't find Matt. A waft of weed and the faint glow of a joint lead me to him.

"What're you doing? I thought you were standing watch."

"I got bored." The soft mango shimmer of his cheeks tells a different story.

"Look, Matt"—I try, with marginal success, to keep the anger from my voice—"I don't know what you did to get on Bryer's bad side, but if you don't want to hunt with me, then please tell me. Don't abandon me with a false sense of security. I hunt very differently by myself."

"David has a crush on you."

"I know." His willingness to share this confidence surprises me. "I'm no threat to you."

"I'm not even sure he likes me sometimes. Maybe he's just interested in someone to pay his rent." After carefully crushing out the joint, he puts it into a case, then snaps it shut and slips it into his pocket. He turns to face me. He's larger than me by a fair amount, but I doubt he'll try to hurt me. Bryer's too powerful, and he depends on the safety being part of her group provides. "And you have more money." A worried saffron blush powders his cheeks. "You threaten me in more ways than just that."

"What do you mean?"

"I never showed David how to stop the bleeding. Corvina did, though. She said *you* showed her."

"Of course, I did. Why didn't you show David?"

He frowns, looks at the ground. "So I could keep him dependent on me, so he wouldn't leave me. But I guess I should have shown him." The fire in his cheeks re-ignites. "After Corvina did, he went around telling everyone about this cool new thing. Bryer's so mad, she can't even talk to me." The heat fades, landing on a soft, but fearful, orange. "I'm afraid she'll kick me out."

"I was afraid she'd kick me out, too. But she didn't."

"What'd you do that was so bad?"

"I told the woman I stay with about me."

"What?" he blurts, his grin incredulous. "You told her?"

"I did. That's when I came to stay with you all." I give him a half-hearted smile. "Bryer won't kick you out. Don't worry about that."

"Your woman's OK with you being ..." He shrugs.

"She's still getting used to the idea." I pat his arm. "Let's go hunt down by the lake before everyone goes home."

We find our next victim at the far end of the dog park. This time, I go first, guiding the man behind a big fir on a side trail. I scrutinize the woods along the sides of the path. So many folks live in the park that even the most remote areas have become vulnerable to prying eyes. After glancing back to ensure Matt's in position, I sink my fangs into the warm flesh. This guy's large enough, so I feed a little longer than I did on the woman. After handing him off, I keep a careful watch, but stay close, mostly to observe Matt. While he does hold his hand over the gash when he finishes, it's not nearly long enough.

"He's still bleeding," I whisper, pressing my hand over the oozing gash.

Matt rolls his eyes. "He'll be fine."

"There's no reason to leave any wound behind. And where are your hand wipes?"

"I don't use them." He licks his hand. "This way, I don't waste anything."

"It's not so much for you." Drawing my hand away, I examine the skin, then wipe everything and let the man go. I hand a packet to Matt—"Wipe your mouth"—then head up the trail. "I need to get to work."

"Wait up." He trots to catch up with me. "Don't you be mad at me, too."

"Of course, I'm mad. Take others besides yourself into consideration." Tempering my anger, I lower my voice.

"You need to be more careful. For everyone's sake. When you're sloppy, it'll come back to bite all of us."

June 20, 2020
Rix

I n the bright early morning light, I gaze at Maggie. Actually, I squint, scooting my stool around the end of the kitchen island so she's no longer backlit by the window. Oh, much better. I could watch her all day. As she languidly stretches, she runs her fingers through her hair, pulling it away from her face. "I'm cutting my hair off."

"Mm-hm," I murmur, then blink. "Um, how short?"

"Just making sure you're paying attention." She smiles mischievously. "It does need trimming. It hasn't been done since before—" She thinks. "Since just before Christmas." She looks at her nails. "The last time I had a manicure, too."

"Is it safe to go in?"

"They're requiring masks and only allowing for twenty-five percent of capacity, but no, not really." She takes a bite of her chocolate croissant. "Would you do it for me? Just the hair." She grins. "I'll make a mess of it."

I run my hand over my head. "Mine's fairly bushy, too. Can we trade?"

"Hmm. That hadn't occurred to me."

Maggie's hair is remarkably difficult to cut. She has so much, and it springs away from me. I learn as I go. Keeping it wet is key. Squirt, comb, clip.

She glows in the attention. "Try to keep it longer in the back and a little shorter over my shoulders."

"I'll try." I snip. "I'm mostly concerned with keeping it even. It's too bouncy."

She giggles. "I'm bouncy."

When I'm done, she plugs in electric clippers. I eye them. "Have you used those before?"

"Once or twice. Definitely better than me trying to do it with scissors." As she works, she hums a familiar song, sings a few of the lyrics, then goes back to humming.

"I recognize that song." Does she know me so well? How long I've suffered? My internal battles?

"'Falling Slowly.'"

"From 'Once.'"

"Right." She smiles. Love her smile. "I watched it again last night. I would've had you come up, but you were out."

"Maybe next time."

She clicks off the clippers, then brushes hair from my neck and removes the towel. "All done. You look good."

The buzz of my phone awakens me. While groping for it on the nightstand, I pull the blanket off my head and squint into the bright afternoon light that makes its way into my room. Four twenty-three. I thumb open my phone.

The text is from Maggie.

> Rama and I are doing game night. Do you want to join us? It will be much better with three playing.

Sounds fun. What time?

> Not til 8:30. But you can come up earlier, if you want. :-) I'm done with work at five, then need to eat and take a shower. So maybe around 7:30?

Will let you know for sure in a bit.

I scroll to Bryer's name.

Is it all right if I skip coming over tonight?

Pulling the blanket over my head, I close my eyes.

My phone vibrates, dragging me from the dozy state between waking and sleep. I sit up and stretch. It's time to rise, regardless. A text awaits me.

> Advanced warning would've been nice.

Bryer's caustic tone comes through.

Sorry. It was last-minute. Is it a problem?

> Don't let it become a habit.

Yes, ma'am.

Don't call me ma'am.

What triggered that?

Won't let it happen again. Thanks. See
you tomorrow.

Listening carefully, I make out the sound of the shower running upstairs. While I wait, I straighten my bed and lay out clothing for the night: my newest pair of jeans; a charcoal button-down sport shirt that I found earlier this year, while I could still get to the used-clothing stores before they closed; clean underwear and socks; and the pair of slippers Maggie bought for me so I don't slip in my stocking feet.

When the shower stops, I text her.

I'm able to come. :-) See you in a bit.

I take extra care washing myself in the shower, wondering if my body odor is significantly different from a breathing person. My new haircut gives me a lot of confidence in my looks. It feels like Maggie cut it fairly evenly. By the time I shave and brush my teeth, it's nearly seven-thirty. I open a tiny brown bottle and pour a few precious drops into my palm. After rubbing my hands together, I smear it on my neck and cheeks. Vanilla. I've always like the way it smells.

When I'm dressed, I feel pretty dapper, except for the slippers. I text Maggie.

Let me know when you're ready.

Now's good.

When I arrive at the landing, the kitchen door stands open.

"In the living room," Maggie calls.

I run my hands over my hair and re-tuck my shirt, then head in. Scattered around, candles burn on every flat surface. Lots of candles. In their soft glow, Maggie sits on the couch, a leopardess lounging in the golden light of sunset. The incandescence of her cheeks exceeds that of the candles. With her hair pulled up into ringlets, she takes my breath away. Literally. My mouth opens, but no air goes in, no words come out.

She smiles. "Say something."

"Uh ... uh ..." I try to inhale, and whisper, "You're so lovely."

"Is that something new?"

"No, but ..."

"Come sit. Let's have some wine." While I get myself settled on the couch next to her, she pours two glasses and hands one to me. "I know rosé is frowned upon in some circles, but I find it refreshing on warm summer nights. You OK with it?"

I softly sing the first few lines from 'Scenes From an Italian Restaurant,' then murmur, "Is this another special occasion?"

"It's the first time we're doing this, so yes. What should *this* toast be?"

"To ... spending time with you." I hold out my glass.

Her tap causes the clarion ring of fine crystal. "To spending time with me."

We both sip.

"Nice. I like it." I take another sip. "I haven't really drunk rosés. You're right. It's refreshing."

"I'm glad." She studies me. "Too bad we can't share a meal."

"Um ..."

"What happens if you eat something?"

"I'd rather not discuss my idiosyncrasies tonight. Can we just drink the wine?"

"I'm sorry. Didn't mean to pry. It's just so fascinating."

"I guess." I take a big swallow, then regret it when she offers me more. I need to be careful. The wine's already provided a buzz. What's the alcohol content? "Sure. A little more, please."

"Sing some more. I like your voice."

I finish out the verse. "I haven't sung much lately. I'm surprised I remember how."

"Thanks. I love that song. It's my favorite Billy Joel." She's glowing. "How's work?"

"Hard to say. India's in a recession due to COVID—it's been pretty bad there—so I'm worried about getting laid off. At the same time, so much of the workforce is out, they need us foreign contractors."

"It's hard to imagine other countries are in worse shape than ours."

"It's no better here. Things are just bad all over. I'm still glad we're in Seattle. It seems like a safer place for you."

She nods. "Probably." At the buzz of her phone, she

sets down her glass, and thumbs it open. "It's Rama. He's ready now. You'll need your phone."

"We're playing online?"

"It's easier than him coming over and me taking him home." She logs into a Zoom meeting. "Hi, Rama." She waves, then angles the computer toward me. "Rix is here."

"Hi." I wave, glad when she moves the camera off me so I don't need to explain why my image is so fuzzy.

"Let's start with a trivia game," Maggie says gleefully. "I'm good at those."

For me, it's hit and miss. I do well on the history questions, and some of the politics and art, but fail miserably on current celebrities and media, especially television. Maggie wins that, hands down. Rama has a good enough general education in American culture, and a really good understanding of world history and events, that he beats me, too. His East African accent is so strong, I sometimes have difficulty understanding him, mostly when the internet cuts in and out for a while, but his obvious intellect and wit can't be stifled. For the first time in such a long time, I'm having fun.

We go on to play a drawing game, which is extremely difficult for me, since my phone doesn't register my finger strokes with any accuracy; another trivia game; and a word game, at which I excel, finally winning at something. Pretty sure I won. Maggie's so competitive, I doubt she'd lose on purpose. Would she?

By ten-thirty, both of them are flagging fast.

"I need to call it a night." Rama's yawn prompts one from Maggie. He quickly covers his mouth with his hand. "Oh, pardon me." His image briefly flares with ruby embarrassment, quickly contained by the Zoom filters. "It was very nice meeting you, Rix. I hope to someday meet in person."

"Maybe soon." I scoot close to Maggie to get my face in the camera. "I enjoyed your company."

"Goodnight, Rama. See you tomorrow night." She clicks *Leave Meeting*. When I shift away, she dreamily murmurs, "Don't move. I like it when you're near me. You smell good, like warm cookies."

"You're tired." I smile. "We should call it a night."

June 29, 2020
Rix

My vibrating phone startles me awake. Rolling to my back, I grope at my pocket to fish it out. I blink at the brightness and make out Nalini's name. Before I can answer, it stops buzzing. Using the dim display for light, I find my laptop wedged under my pillow. The glare from its screen when I crack it open is too much. I close it. Rubbing my face doesn't push away the grogginess. I fumble for the lamp on the nightstand, and keep my eyes closed until they adjust.

What was I working on? I drag myself to sitting, plunk the computer on my lap and open it. Oh, right. Waiting for that machine to restore itself, and trying to figure out why it went down.

Pulling out my phone, I click Nalini's text.

Hey. Lini here. Phone me, OK?

What could be so important it warrants a call? It can't be this ticket. I glance at the time—one-thirty AM, so early afternoon in Mumbai. Texting's tempting, but I click the phone icon, and review the job status while I wait.

"Hello, John." Nalini's voice is melodic. "Did I wake you?"

"No," I mumble. My brain's still foggy. "Beta Cephei's just running through some validation. Oh, there it goes. All green. I assume that's what you're calling about."

"Yes. And no."

The keys rattle on my keyboard. Here it comes. "What else?" I try to make my fingers stop.

"I've got a surprise for you." She sounds cheerful enough.

"I hope it's a good one." I hate long, drawn out dismissals. Maybe she'll give me a good referral.

"The company's making some layoffs." My stomach drops. At least, now I know. "And it means," she continues, "that more of the work's shifting here to India." I wish she'd just spit it out. "You've always been so reliable, we hate the thought of losing you." Is she intentionally trying to make this more painful? "We're letting go all of the American team below the lead level."

"Thanks for letting me know," I manage.

"Oh, no no. We want to make you a lead. Well, I want to make you a lead, and I convinced Rakesh. It'll mean some additional responsibilities. You'll have a mixture of seven employees and contractors reporting to you. But you'll no longer need to monitor systems, just the people who monitor them. You'll need to become a regular salaried employee."

"I ... I don't know what to say," I stammer. This is not a job I'd normally choose.

"You'll make a good lead. Everyone likes you. And you'll even get a raise and a little signing bonus. Are you happy now?"

"Of course. Thank you." I can always back out later. "When does this change take place?"

"In two weeks. Sorry to say, in the meantime, you'll need to do a lot of orientation virtually. If it wasn't for the virus, we'd be flying you out for on-site training, but for now, we'll need to wait to meet in person."

"I would've liked that." That would've been a deal breaker. I'm not certain this change isn't. It's much better than nothing, though. "Hey. Do you think it'd be OK for me to take a week off between now and then? I could use a break before starting new responsibilities."

"Oh, most definitely. I'll send you the offer and all the paperwork to fill out. There'll be several Zoom calls, but other than that, your time's your own. No need to work on any new tickets. Besides, don't you have a national holiday coming up?" She's certainly not a woman of few words. "Let me know if you have any questions. I'll let you go now. Get some sleep."

"Thanks. I will." I'm happy for the time off. I need to get in some serious hunting. My hunger's the likely cause of this lethargy. I suspect I'm anemic, but it's not like I can see a doctor about it. I just need to feed more often. And sleep.

After closing the ticket, I set my computer on the

nightstand. With a click, the room is dark. Dropping to the bed, I roll to my side. I should get undressed, but my eyes are already shut.

June 30, 2020
Rix

The buzz of my phone draws me awake. I blink into the brightness of the display. Seven AM. A text from Maggie awaits me.

> You up? Let's have coffee.

> Give me five to wash up. :-)

I tug off the shirt I fell asleep in and pull on a new one, then hurry to the bathroom to wash my face. Running my fingers through my hair, I feel for places where it may be sticking out at weird angles. Less chance now that Maggie trimmed it. I head up the stairs. After rapping lightly on the kitchen door, I let myself in. The scent of brewing coffee wafts from the gurgling coffeemaker.

Maggie enters and walks right past me. "Good morning." After filling a cup, she turns. "You look tired." She gives me the once over—being a nurse, she probably can't help herself—and offers me the cup. "Up all night again?"

Taking the steaming mug, I breathe in the aroma. "Actually, no." I take a sip. "Oh, this is good." I give her a smile. "I got a promotion, which changed my job responsibilities so I ended up sleeping for a few hours."

After filling a cup for herself and adding a splash of milk, she sits on the stool across from me. "Then, why the dark circles?" I set my cup down. The coffee makes my empty stomach churn. Her fingers brush my hand. "Are you all right? I can't tell."

I shrug. "Vampire." When her eyes drop, I regretfully stammer, "I ... I'm sorry. I shouldn't be so flippant."

"I can't imagine what it's like for you." She swirls the liquid.

I sing the opening to 'Maggie May,' using my best Rod Stewart impression. This works. I get a smile.

"I love those old songs." Her dark eyes shine. "Especially that one. You have such a nice voice."

"Thanks." To keep my fingers from drumming the countertop, I pretend to sip my coffee. "Things have been kind of rough for me lately. It's been hard finding enough" —I nearly say *victims*—"to eat. With the virus and everything. I'm constantly hungry." My eyes wander. When my gaze returns to Maggie, her face shows revulsion. She goes back to swirling her coffee. I set my cup down. "This isn't easy to talk about. It's not something even you should know."

"I'm glad you told me," she says softly, then raises her eyes. I'll never tire of gazing into her eyes. "How's that work? I mean, how do you eat?" She purses her lips. "Do you hypnotize people?" Her eyes grow large. "Do you kill them?"

"No. Of course not." My croaking voice sounds defensive, even to me. "It's hard to explain."

"I'm listening."

"I'm very careful not to kill my"—my knee begins to shake, but I make it stop—"victims."

She studies me. "Have you ever killed someone?" My mouth opens. I have no more breath to speak. I close it and look down at my hands. She slips off her stool—"I see"—and takes her cup to the sink. "I don't know what to do with this."

Running water fills the silence. It overflows to muffle the sound of her sniffles. She does not hear, or at least does not react, to my approach. The bright sunshine in the yard outside the window makes me squint. I put my cup next to hers, move the tap to fill it, then turn it off. Her tears follow the last of the water gurgling down the drain. The rise and fall of her chest is the only movement. Her breath, the only sound.

"Maggie?" I say, barely a whisper. I slide my hand along the edge of the sink until it makes contact with hers.

She turns her head toward me for a moment before putting her focus on her yard. "Why are you here?"

"Do you mean standing here, next to you by the sink?" That causes her to look at me. I can't read her expression. "Or, here in Seattle?" Her moue tells me that's not it. I grimace. "Or, here ... in general?" A tiny nod confirms that one. "I don't know. Who would've thought vampires were real?" She hasn't moved her hand, so I guess she's still not afraid of me. I'll try to keep it that way. "I lead a complicated existence. I didn't mean to drag you into it."

"Answer one question for me." Her little finger slips over mine, pinning me in place. "I need you to tell me the truth."

"I would *never* lie to you." I'm uncertain it's possible for me to lie to her. Does she possess her own magics?

"Is what I feel for you real?"

"Um ..." I wasn't expecting that.

"Tell me, Rix," she goes on, voice intense, gaze unwavering. "Am I hypnotized or under some spell?"

"No, Maggie." I shake my head. Could she be? "I'd never intentionally control you."

"All right." Her ring finger nudges her pinky over one more. "I believe you. Let's go back to your first response."

"Why am I here with you?" My eyes search her face for the answer. "It's not like I was looking for a relationship. I never thought one could be within my reach. But you ..."

Her fingers move like a mini-tsunami until her pinky captures my thumb. Our eyes lock. Her lips part. Can this be happening? Do I want this to happen? My hand gets pulled along with hers as she turns toward me. The heat of her breath wafts like a gentle desert wind on my cheek. The embers of her lips burn into my flesh, branding me as her own. She whispers in my ear, "Some souls are destined to be together."

July 1, 2020
Rama

I arrive at the ER to face another short-staffed night. After running my eyes down the roster, I glance up at Althea's deep brown face. Her countenance, her entire bearing, exhibits her fatigue. Her crinkled eyes must indicate a smile, but it looks more like a grimace. "I'm working on it."

"I'm not complaining."

"I know, my friend." Her chest rises and falls with her deep breath. "You would be the last person to ever complain."

A couple of hours later, from behind me I hear a cheerful, "Hi, Rama. I hoped you'd be here."

"Maggie." I turn. "So good to see your smiling face, even if I can't see your smile."

"Short again, I hear."

"The holiday weekend on top of summer vacations and, well, COVID's not going away any time soon." I wait as she checks in. "The only good to come of it is I get to see you more often."

"Did you hear? The state hit nearly eight hundred today. That's as bad as at the peak back in April. Maybe worse. And it's on an upward slope."

"The Second Wave." Not wanting to break Maggie's good mood, I intentionally change the subject. "How are things with Rix?"

She looks down and away. A rosy blush touches her cheeks. "Moving along." She brings her eyes up to mine. "He had fun playing games with us. We should do it again sometime."

"We should get together for dinner some night. I'd like to meet him in person." That request makes me feel fatherly, but I do hold familial affection for her.

"He's out most nights, and he also works at night." Above her mask, her eyes pinch slightly and the blush returns to her cheeks. "But I'll ask." Is she making up excuses for him? Something strange is going on, but I can't put my finger on it. An alert pops up. Her eyes dart to the monitor. "Ah, we're off. I'm on this one." She seems relieved to dash out. Is she avoiding me?

We go fairly non-stop until a quarter to ten, when I hand off the last of the current cases to the hospital for admittance. As I scrub, Maggie appears beside me. "Time to eat. Hungry?" she asks. "It's Japanese tonight."

It feels good to sit. The steaming miso soup doesn't hurt. I dig into the tonkatsu and rice with my little plastic fork, but Maggie deftly snatches up the juicy tidbits, and even the sticky white rice, with her chopsticks. I need to learn to use them. Between bites, I ask, "Any plans this weekend?"

"I hadn't really thought that far ahead. It's supposed to be cool and damp."

"There's that. And the fireworks were canceled."

"Well, the protests aren't likely to go away. Things seem to be heating up." She stops eating to look off into the distance.

I glance over my shoulder, but see nothing out of the ordinary. "Maggie." Her gaze returns to me. "Don't forget to eat. Have you tried the eggplant?"

"Nasu Dengaku. One of my favorites." She's back to smiling. "Dad used to take me to a little hole-in-the-wall called Maneki, just off Jackson." Her smile fades. "I wonder how they'll survive the pandemic."

"Perhaps we can eat there sometime. Or at least get take out." I scoop up a sauce-laden spoonful of rice. "This sauce is so good. All the food is."

"It is. I haven't had Japanese in forever." She bites a

gyoza in half then dips the remainder into a little container of the vinegary sauce and chomps it down. "Mmm. Now, I'm full."

"We should get back to it."

We're busy again until after eleven, when we both return to the nurses' station. I lean on the counter, my elbow touching her hand, the first physical contact we've had in months. We're standing too close. I move a meter or so away. Her stifled yawn elicits one in me. "Don't yawn," I chide. "I need to be here four more hours."

"Sorry. At least my first patient tomorrow isn't until ten-thirty." She may be attempting a smile behind her mask, but it doesn't reach her tired eyes. "I get to sleep in a little."

"Do you get to see Rix at all?" How'd that slip out? I'm more tired than I realized. "I'm sorry. That's none of my business."

"That's all right. He sometimes has coffee with me in the morning and we talk: weather; the pandemic; politics. He's the only one I go in depth with. We're too busy here."

"That sounds nice. So you two worked out your differences?"

"I'd say, we're still working on that." This time, her eyes do smile. "We're taking it slow and easy."

"I'll quit worrying, then."

She reaches a hand to my arm. "Don't do that."

2

CHAOS

July 3, 2020
Rix

After reading the same sentence three times, I rub my eyes and scroll to see how much remains in this training module. Four more pages. Could they make it any more boring? Amber light on the rug near the window slowly creeps across the living room toward me. I may need to draw the shade. Since I've been spending so much time upstairs in the evenings, my eyes seem to be adapting to more light. It's something I never thought to try.

Tonight, I can finally go out hunting by myself. It's also a holiday, so there should be lots of idiots out blowing things up. I can't go much longer without feeding. It's already been too long.

In her room upstairs, Maggie has been quiet for the past quarter of an hour. She must have finished for the day. Good. Maybe we can spend some time together before I leave. Her feet padding down the stairs tell me she's coming. I rise, squinting through the brightness at the doorway. The sunlight creates an effective wall to keep me from crossing the room. She comes in and gives me a curious expression, then glances at the rug and over at the window. "Why didn't you just pull the shade?" She tugs the cord. The room dims.

"I was caught up in my reading." I smile when she turns toward me. "I didn't notice until it was too late. Long day. Are you finished?"

"With my patients." She comes to the couch and sits sideways, then pats the cushion, waiting until I sit facing her. "I'm going out to the protests tonight. You should come."

"I ... um ... was reading these docs." I need to go hunting.

"We could use someone with your training. You've been a great asset." She touches my knee. "Jandal and Emily both tested positive, so they can't come, and we're expecting a busy night."

"Things got worse?"

"The tension's been growing since they closed the CHOP on Wednesday. Rumors say the Proud Boys will be here tonight, and people arriving from all over the country to join them."

"I read about that." Another clear and present danger for me to avoid. Plus, they're limiting my hunting grounds. "Maybe you should stay home. You worked a full day. And it's a holiday. When's the last time you took a night off?"

"I can't stay home. They're already short-handed." She

moves her fingers to my hand. "I'll feel safer if you're there with me."

"All right. I'll go with you." What did I just say? How does she do that?

She gets up. "Come chat with me while I eat." After shoving my laptop under the couch, I follow her to the kitchen. She pops a freezer meal into the microwave, then comes to sit across from me. "Tell me what's happening. I haven't had a chance to look today."

"Well, you already heard the Proud Boys rumor, but there's no evidence of huge numbers of outsiders descending on the city. They must have lost interest after the CHOP closed, so that's actually a good thing to come of it. I think they all opted to go to Mt Rushmore to hear the President speak tomorrow instead."

"That should heat things up, as if they weren't already about to explode." When the timer dings, she jumps, then rises to retrieve her dinner. "Keep going."

"Um. Let's see. Oh, he wasn't very happy when de Blasio okayed painting *Black Lives Matter* in huge yellow letters on Fifth Avenue." I wait for Maggie to sit and get situated. "He tweeted it would be 'denigrating this luxury Avenue.' de Blasio called the President's tweets 'the definition of racism.'" I grin. "They're sparring."

"Someone needs to spar with him." She pushes some chunks of what might be chicken around in a syrupy crimson sauce, and grunts. "What else?"

"You really want me to keep going?" She doesn't need all of this, but I can't think of anything positive. When she nods, I add, "Well, The United Nations Human Rights Council debated launching a special investigation of racism in America after the killing of George Floyd. I doubt it'll go anywhere, but it tells the story of how the rest of the world views us."

"Hmm. Maybe we should emigrate to Canada." She smiles, making her eyes sparkle like black opals. "Or New Zealand. I've always wanted to visit there."

"With your background, you'd be welcome in either place. After the borders reopen."

"Oh. I guess New Zealand isn't really an option for you."

"It would be nearly impossible to get there. Maybe in the bowels of a ship." A memory of working in the galley of a commercial fishing vessel back in the fifties flits through my mind—when the US Army caught up with me for the last time. Escaping onto the boat was a safer option than being taken into custody. "And, with no passport, I can't enter Canada."

A confused whirlpool of emotions eddies around her face. Taking another bite of her meal, she chews slowly, then swallows. "This food's hardly worth eating, especially after being spoiled at the ER with Meals for Heroes, but it's a shame to just throw it out." I'd hate for her to waste it, too. As it cools, the sauce congeals into something resembling blood. She purses her lips, takes another bite. A drop dribbles down her chin, looking even more like blood. My stomach rumbles, but she doesn't seem to notice. "I should learn to cook, but I don't really have time."

I want to say, 'I can teach you,' but decide against it and hand her a napkin. "I guess we'll be out all night. I hope you're planning to rest tomorrow."

"It's Saturday. And the Fourth of July. I can sleep during the day." She squints her eyes at me. "Just like you."

July 3 to 4, 2020
Rix

Maggie drives us to the same driveway she parked at the last time I joined her at a protest. It's nearly ten by the time we arrive. This time, she leads me toward the backyard.

"Maggie." I stop. "Can you just pick up the supplies again while I wait in the car? I'm not sure I feel comfortable with this. Maybe someone will ... notice me."

"Oops. I haven't forgotten in months. You distract me." As she digs into her bag, she smiles. She's ignoring my question. "Here, put on a mask. You'll be fine." She loops hers behind her ears and bends the wire over her nose. When she looks at me, her eyes crinkle, but I can't see her grin. She adjusts my mask. "After all these months, haven't you figured out how to wear these properly?" She starts down the path along the side of the house. "Let's go. The others are probably already waiting."

Beyond the gate, about a dozen people, all in masks, stand alone or in small, properly distanced groups. Some wear orange vests with *MEDIC* printed in large white letters, but most just have red masking tape crosses on their shoulders, backs and chests, and the occasional white skateboarding helmet or hardhat. Maggie checks in with a tall, black-haired woman holding a clipboard, and returns with an assignment sheet and a roll of tape. She seems to take pleasure in decorating me, and in having me return the favor.

A brown-skinned man with short black hair dashes up to the woman with the clipboard, checks in and hurriedly tapes himself in red crosses before scanning the crowd. When he spots Maggie, his eyes smile, surrounded by an affectionate amber glow. He approaches, but stops an arm span away. Over the growing din of the group, he shouts to be heard through his mask, "Althea said I should join you. Thanks for waiting." His East African accent identifies him as Rama. "I was caught up in an emergency. And you know how small our crews are these days."

"I'm so glad you're here. Now, there's three of us." Maggie glances at me over her shoulder. "I brought Rix. He has some EMT experience. Rix, this is Rama, in the flesh. I don't know if I told you, he's from Tanzania." She pronounces it with the emphasis equally weighted on the first two syllables, just like a Tanzanian medic I worked alongside way back in the seventies. I like that she pays attention to such details.

For an awkward moment, he studies me, with ochre-dusted cheeks, full of curiosity, but then his brown eyes smile. Reaching out his hand, he mocks a handshake. "Good to meet you in person." I return the gesture.

"OK, people. Listen up," Althea yells. Everyone stops talking. "It may be a wild one tonight. Don't get separated. Call if anything goes wrong, and I'll try to send a backup team. Stay safe. Let's go."

"We're the Interstate 5 team," Maggie says.

"I-5?" I ask.

"Didn't you hear it in the news? Protests have been happening on the freeway every night for nearly three weeks. The State Patrol's shutting it down now." She herds us to a van parked in the alley behind the yard, and clicks open the locks. "They try to keep it safe."

"I'll ride in back"—I slide open the side door—"so you two can plan."

Once we're on our way, with all the windows fully open, I look behind the seat. Costco-sized packs of bottled water line one side. Several large bins line the other. Two bulging backpacks sit on the floor between them.

"It looks well stocked," I shout, but neither hears me. I don't have enough breath to be good at shouting.

When we arrive, the State Patrol allows us onto the freeway. Maggie parks straddling the shoulder and the first lane to help shield protesters from unauthorized traffic. The lights of downtown sparkle beyond the several lanes wide road. I peer around, feeling exposed out in the open, searching for cover, finding none. I focus on Maggie, who's managing our set up. Helping her eases some of my discomfort.

While she finishes double-checking both packs, the first of the protesters arrive. Initially, they mill around, finding friends, making certain everyone has a mask and sharing stories of the march earlier tonight. I can smell them. Most of them are healthy. My stomach growls. Their words envelop me in fragmented sentences: "... pepper-sprayed right in the face ..."; "... thanks for the pizza ..."; "... cops didn't stop them ..."; "... Jen had to work ..."; "... sure it was the Proud Boys ... ."

A tinny voice from a megaphone overpowers the cacophony. I don't hear what's said. I huddle next to our van, shifting from foot to foot, wanting to disappear. When the singing begins, reminiscent of the sixties, some of the tension leaves my shoulders, but the echoing noises still overwhelm me. The scintillating lights of a police car dance from the retaining walls and vehicles, giving me no single place to land my eyes. I close them, and wish for it all to stop.

When someone touches my arm, I spring away.

Maggie studies me. "What's wrong?"

"I'm fine." I whimper, then take a breath to regain control of my voice. "I zoned out. I'm just tired. And maybe a little anxious."

"I don't have a good feeling tonight, either." She moves to examine me more closely. "Are you sure you're OK?"

I nod.

As Rama opens the second package of water bottles at the back of the van, the crowd beyond him erupts with shouts of "Car! Car!" The roar of an engine draws my eyes to a white Jaguar racing up the empty freeway. Tires squeal as it swerves around our van, heading straight for the protesters.

July 4, 2020
Rix

The sky to the northeast glows a pale, milky shade by the time we arrive back at Maggie's. We strip down to our underwear by the door and take turns scrubbing our arms and faces in the powder room near the kitchen. Maggie slips into a robe she pulls from behind the door. As we collapse onto the couch, she takes my hand. The fabric of her wrap's cool and silky where it touches my leg. "I'm sorry."

"For what?"

"For dragging you into that chaos."

"No, Maggie. I was all right. I'm happy I was there to support you."

She drops her head to my shoulder. With me in my current state, how can I tolerate the contact? And why does it have to feel so comfortable? All too soon, she lifts it. "I should shower, and maybe eat something. And then, I need some sleep." She kisses my cheek. "Thanks for sitting with me." Standing, she tugs on my hand.

When I try to rise, my head swims. I get halfway up before dropping back to the couch. What's going on? Oh. Oh no!

"Rix, what's wrong?" Kneeling in front of me, she puts her hand on my forehead. Her palm is hot. Her blood pulses against my skin.

"That won't tell you anything," I mutter.

"Are you getting sick? *Can* you get sick?"

"Not that I'm aware of." My stomach rumbles and churns. I'd be all right if I could only feed. But things keep getting in my way. "I ... um ... I haven't had anything to eat in a very long time." I close my eyes. "Maybe too long." I let my head drop back to the cushion, away from her hand. "You go shower. We'll see how I feel when you're done."

She stands and studies me with a worried frown. "All right."

As soon as she's gone, I text Bryer.

> Are you up? I have a problem.

I close my eyes as I wait for the response.
A minute—or maybe ten—passes. My phone vibrates.

> What's wrong?

> Need blood. Waited too long. Don't know what to do.

> Some pig's blood is best. Gonna be hard to find at this time of day. I'll see if Matt has any snacks left. Hold on.

How long does she expect me to wait? My knee begins to bounce. I let it. Finally, another text arrives.

> Where are you? Cleve can still bring some on his bike before sunrise, if you're not too far.

The shower stops.

> Let me talk to my roommate.

Maggie comes down the stairs dressed in shorts and a tank top, with a towel around her head. "How're you doing?"

"Not well. I ... um ..." I stammer, "really need some blood." Her eyes grow large. I hold up my hands. "No no no. Not *your* blood."

"Whose, then?"

"A pig's. The place where I was staying, they have a container, but ..." My knee resumes its hyperactivity. "I didn't want to tell them where you live."

"How will you get it?"

"I don't know. I don't have time to walk over there ... before the sun." I probably can't walk that far, regardless.

"Where is it?"

"Just two blocks from the picnic area at the park. Near where you picked me up that one time."

"What happens if you don't get it?"

I can't look at her. "Um ... I don't know what to do." My anxiety rises. I can barely sit still. "Um ... If you drive me over, I might be able to get inside before sunrise. But then, I'll need to stay there for the day."

"I'd rather have you here, so I can monitor you." Sitting beside me, she places her hand on my knee to still it. It pulses on my bare skin. "Would I be safe"—she tries to peer into my face, but I keep my head down—"if I went to get it for you?"

I look into her eyes. "I'd never ask that of you."

"What alternative do we have?" She raises her brows. How can she stay so calm? Oh. Right. She *is* a nurse. "Can they bring it to the corner where I picked you up? And just hand it through the window?"

Relief floods me, allowing me to take a full breath. "I'll tell Bryer you're on your way, and ask her to send Cleve with it. You'll be safe with him." I put my hand over hers and give it a squeeze. "Thank you."

Twenty minutes later, Maggie returns and holds out a jar to me.

"Would you please warm it?" I try not to stare at it. "Body temperature. Like a baby bottle? Don't let it get hot spots or it'll cook."

She goes to heat it in the microwave. When the timer chimes, she calls, "Should I put this in a cup?"

"It's fine the way it is."

"They sent two, so I put one in the fridge." Maggie sits next to me. "Do you need help?"

"Maybe." As she holds the container to my lips, I put my hand over hers and give it a little tug when I need to stop, like that first night with Corvina. She pulls it away slightly. I reach for it. "I can manage now." I drink the rest of the contents.

She stays beside me until I'm done. "Some color's returned to your cheeks." Her voice sounds sterile and clinical. "Do you feel any better?" I nod. She takes the jar. "Let's get you settled. I need to eat. And get some laundry going. I'm totally out of clothes. And then, I need to get some sleep. Text if you need me."

July 4, 2020
Rix

I'm having such a strange dream. It must be a dream. It's too bright to be real. I'm in a large, loud crowd. Surrounded by concrete. We're in a basement? No, we're outside. I don't know why I'm here. I call for Maggie. I can't find her. "Maggie. Maggie. Oh, no. No no no."

"Rix, wake up."

Blinking open my eyes, I squint into late afternoon light that spills in around the living room window blind. "Why am I on the couch?"

Maggie sits on the edge of the cushion beside me. "What were you dreaming?"

"It was strange. We were outside, but maybe it was daytime. Why would I be outside in the daylight?"

"What else? You called my name. You sounded afraid."

"A car. There was a car. And you were kneeling in its path. Right in the sun. I couldn't get to you." I push myself to sitting. "Why am I on the couch?"

"You were more out of it than I thought. How do you feel?"

"Oh, I remember. We went to the protest. Those people"—I take a shaky breath—"*they* were on the ground. Are they all right?"

"One's stable." Maggie looks at her hands. Tears well in her eyes. "The other's in critical condition and may not make it." Two tears leave wet traces on her cheeks. I have no comforting words. I place my hand over hers. She pulls away, then moves down the couch to sit facing me. "The world's gone mad."

I cross my legs so I can scoot closer to her. "It does that sometimes. It can be a hard place to live in."

She frowns. "I guess you've lived through a lot."

"A world war. A pandemic. The Twenties. A depression. The rise of fascism." I look away. "I survived another world war." I return my eyes to hers. "The Fifties. The Sixties ... And now, I'm back to the Twenties. And another pandemic. It feels like history's repeating itself."

"That gives you a different perspective. A longer-term view. You didn't answer my question, though. How do you feel now that you've had ..." She makes a face.

"It helps a little." I edge closer to Maggie, until my knees bump against hers. She doesn't recoil, so that's good. "I don't normally go this long without ... human blood."

Her gaze flits around my face, avoiding my eyes. "Would it help ... if you bit me? Would it hurt?"

My brows shoot up. "I'd never, ever do that to you."

"Would it make me into—"

"No. There's a lot more to it than that."

"Are all of you so restrained?"

"Unfortunately, no. It takes self-control. The younger ones, in particular, didn't have a chance to develop that fully before ..." My voice trails off, and my eyes wander. "Imagine being forever twenty, with a twenty-year-old's mind. Or worse, a teenager. But that same lack of impulse control usually means they don't survive for long."

"It's kind of ironic." Maggie's soft voice draws my attention back to her.

"In a way, I was lucky, already an adult with a strong set of morals. And, aside from the sin of stealing me from my wife and daughter … well, there were way more sins than just that"—I look at my hands—"the person who did this to me provided some instruction."

Tears slip down Maggie's cheeks. "I'm so sorry, Rix," she whispers. "I didn't know about your family."

I touch her hand. "There's no way you could have even imagined it."

"They were who your paper boats were for."

"Mm-hm," I murmur, "they were."

July 8 to 9, 2020
Corvina

I'm getting way better at Bejeweled. I made it! I'm a Topaz Hunter. I check the time. Ten-forty-five. It's barely dark outside. I used to love the long summer days, but now I hate them. Rix isn't coming tonight. He's *working*. Everyone else is already out hunting, except David and Matt, who're making their bed squeak downstairs. I'm so bored. I want someone to talk to. Even if it's David.

After pulling on a tank top and shorts—I mostly quit wearing clothes in my room so I don't have to wash them so much—I slip out the window. I don't care what Rix says. I'm going to Woodland Park. It's Wednesday, but people are still wandering around when I go in at the parking lot behind the tennis courts and head up a path into the woods.

I smell weed before hearing a low whistle. Cheugy

older guys. No one my age would do that. I wiggle my butt —*that* should get them going—and continue along the trail.

A boy, probably a little older than me, appears out of the bushes. "Hi."

"Hi." I smile, but keep walking.

He walks beside me. "You shouldn't be out here alone."

"Will ya protect me?" I take his hand. That's strange. It's cold, even though the night is warm. We head into the maze of trails between the lake and the lawn bowling, whatever that means. At a fork, he tugs me up the hill. I stop. "I don't like goin' to the encampment. Too many people. Someone might recognize me."

He rolls his eyes. "Like who?"

"That man who let me stay in his tent." Back before I got sick—and met Erlandr. "It was pourin', and I was soaked and freezin' cold. He tol' me to git outta those wet things."

"You stripped for him?"

"He gave me a shirt to wear, and a blanket to wrap up in. Then, he gave me a Snickers and a Coke. He was nice enough, but figured I'd be better off back home." Why would I want to go there after Buddy—? I miss my mom, and Linda and Kylie. I blink away tears. "I barely escaped the next mornin' before CPS showed up."

"Don't blame ya. I landed in foster care for a while." He makes a face. "Now I'm out here. I got some weed." He smiles. "Let's go light up." On a barely visible trail, he leads me into the ravine and behind some large shrubs. Under the branches, it's clear, like a little cave.

"Nice. Do ya live here?"

"Sorta. Sometimes." He plops down and pulls out a joint and lighter. After taking a drag, he holds it out to me. "Here," he croaks, trying to hold in the smoke.

"I like it better this way." I straddle him and put my lips over his. He exhales into my mouth. Slipping down, I sit in his lap. He puts his arms around me. It feels nice to be held. "What's your name?"

"Teddy."

"I'm Corvina. Let's do some more."

Rix told me drugs don't affect us like regular humans, but this makes me feel nice. We keep smoking til there's almost nothing left. He tamps it out in the dirt, then flicks the filter into the bushes.

"How ya feelin'?" He smiles.

My head swims. I hope his is, too. I lean forward until he topples to his back, and kiss him. I really like the feel of my tongue against his. I move my mouth to his neck and lick it. Something isn't right. I'm not getting the usual buzz and my fangs won't come out. I lift my head to look at him. "You're a vampire."

He rolls me to my back, pinning me to the ground. "You're right." He nips my neck.

"Ow," I giggle, "stop that."

His mouth drops open before his fangs disappear. "You, too?" He starts giggling with me. "This is so weird." He pushes himself to sitting. "I wasted a whole joint on you."

As I sit up, I playfully punch him in the shoulder, remembering not to hit too hard. "Ya didn't waste it. Ya git to spend time with me."

He gets real serious. "How long ya been ... like this?"

"A few months. What about you?"

"Not even that long. At least, I'm not always hungry anymore."

"Yeah. Me, too. How is it, hangin' out here?"

"Hard to stay outta the sun all day. I'm gettin' kinda tired of it."

"So it's true. I thought Rix told me that just to keep me from goin' out in the daytime."

"Who's Rix?"

"A guy I know." I doodle in the dirt. "He found me a place to stay."

"That'd be nice."

"I dunno," I mutter. "They boss me around and won't let me go out when I want."

"Better'n bein' out here alone." He looks sad.

"What else hasn't Rix told me?"

"Wha'd'ya mean?"

"Well, right after it happened, I tried to kill myself." I give him a sideways glance. "I cut my wrist." I show him the scar, but it's almost gone. "He told me that wouldn't work. That I wouldn't be able to kill myself. I just believed him."

"I tried that, too." His voice gets quiet. "I'm just so lonely." Now, he looks *really* sad.

"I wonder what else kills vampires. Maybe wooden stakes, like on Buffy."

Teddy nods. "If you get it in the heart, you go poof."

Looking around, I find a broken branch with a pointy end. "Like this one?" I press the tip to my chest, then turn it around. The other end's pretty sharp, too.

"Don't do that." He grabs my wrist. "Put it down. We're havin' a good time, aren't we?"

After I drop it, I push him to the ground and kiss him again. "Will ya hold me?"

He wraps an arm around me. "I could do more, if you want." His hand strokes my body as he slips up my tank top.

Sitting up, I open the buttons on his shirt. The pointy stick catches my eye. He presses himself against my crotch. I lean forward onto my hands and lower myself to his body. The skin on his chest is cool against my tits. My hand lands on the broken stick. I wrap my fingers around it. Can I make it go through both our hearts at the same time? When I sit back, he slides his hands inside my shorts, but I don't want anyone touching me there. I put one end of the stick against my chest, and fall forward.

July 9, 2020
Erlandr

Across the ravine, I spot a young couple. "That's Corvina," I whisper to Azul, "with a boy."

"Dios mío, let her have some fun."

"She's not supposed to be out by herself. I told her I'd take her hunting tomorrow."

"I don't know how you'll get over there, let alone find the way down." Azul tugs on my sleeve. "Let's go. I'm hungry."

I'm hungry, too, but I'm responsible for her. "Do you mind hunting alone? I need to go get her."

"Oh, all right." She sounds just like David, or even Corvina. "Do what you need to do. Good luck dragging her away." She stomps off down the trail toward the lake.

I study the trees, spotting a big fir that splits into two about halfway up and use that as a landmark. Staying as close as I can to the gully, I follow several dead ends and trails so overgrown with blackberries that I need to double back. This is the wildest part of the entire park. Finally, one path leads to the marker tree. The lingering smell of weed guides me closer.

"Will ya hold me?" That's definitely Corvina.

As I move toward her voice, I enter a small clearing and find her face down on a patch of light grey dirt. "What did you do?" I rasp, trying to keep my voice quiet.

"Tried to kill us." She brushes ash from her chest and belly, and tugs on her shirt. "I only got Teddy."

I jerk her to her feet. Rustling in the bushes on the far side grabs my attention. I catch sight of the back of someone scrambling up another path. "Dammit, Corvina. Someone saw you."

"Ow. You're hurtin' me." She struggles to get away, but I'm stronger.

"Keep your voice down. Let's get out of here." When she keeps fighting me, I get my arm around her waist and drag her up the hill.

"Lemme go." She flails her arms and kicks her feet, landing a few good blows on my shins.

"Shut up." When we get to the top, I grab her by both

arms. "What's wrong with you? Do you want to get us all killed?"

"I don't care," she says so calm and cool it causes a chill to run up my spine.

"Saving you was my biggest mistake." Letting go of one arm, I keep a firm grip on the other. "I don't even know if we should go home. That man'll probably talk to the cops."

July 9, 2020
Rix

My new job requires a lot more of my time, at least right now, as I'm getting to know my new team. Bryer grudgingly let me work from Maggie's tonight after being insistent I work at her house on my first three nights. I have one more employee call and I'll have talked to everyone. Was taking this position a mistake? No one likes that I require audio-only calls, but I can understand that. I press dial.

Twenty minutes in, a text alert pops up from Bryer.

Get your ass over here right now.

I'm glad this meeting isn't video, so Lekha can't see me typing.

What's going on?

"I understand your concerns, Lekha. I'm here to support you, not to undermine you."

"I just wanted to put that out there at the beginning." Her voice drops. "It's hard being a woman in this field, and I wasn't happy about moving away from Nalini. But I am excited about her promotion."

Corvina was seen staking a boy she met at the park.

Be there as soon as I can.

"I'm looking forward to working with you. I've heard only good things about you. Just know that I'm on your side. And you can contact me anytime you need me."

"Thanks, John."

"I'll let you get back to work. Talk to you soon."

I head out. Worry clouds my thoughts, but I try not to dwell on it until I get there and learn more—one of the ways my mother taught me to deal with my anxiety. As soon as I open the door, Bryer's on her feet, face flaming her rage. Before she can start yelling, I ask, "Where is she?" She points at Corvina's door. Going in, I find her sitting at the head of the bed with her arms crossed over her dirty, bloodied shirt. Erlandr sits on the chair near the door. Standing guard? I meet his eyes. "I'll take over."

As he rises to leave, weariness hangs on him, dragging down his shoulders, making his feet scuff on the floor. "Do you want the door closed?"

"Please." Taking his place, I scoot closer to face the sullen girl. "Tell me what happened. I want to hear it from you first."

"I was bored. No one was around, well, except for Matt and David, who I guess were here to babysit me, but they were going at it like bunnies in the basement. So I went out."

"And?" I prompt. A kaleidoscope of colors swirl around her. She's always full of mixed emotions, so never easy to read.

"I met this boy, but he was a vampire too. And he was all alone and really sad. We got stoned. Really baked. I found this stick and wondered if I could kill both of us at once." Her voice fades. "Then Erlandr was there and he was so mad." Tears pool in her eyes. Her aura locks on verdant grief. "I hate it when he's mad at me. But there was someone else and I didn't know they were there, but they musta saw us." She looks up at me. "I didn't know they were there. It's not my fault."

"I'm sorry I wasn't here for you tonight. I thought someone would look after you. Bryer's got every right to throw you out, you know. And Erlandr. And me."

"You don't live here, anyways." She sneers. "You left us to go stay with some woman."

"I did. I should have stayed here. You're my responsibility."

"I'm Erlandr's responsibility. *He* made me."

I don't want to turn this into an argument. "Why's your shirt so dirty? And why is it bloody?"

"I landed on Teddy, or what was left of him. Did you know we turn to ashes? The stick cut me instead of killin' me, too."

So, staking does work. I'd only heard second-hand

accounts, where it's hard to differentiate myth from reality. "Let me see your wound."

Before I can protest, she tugs off her tank. This child has no modesty. I look away. "Please, cover your breasts."

"Pfft." She smirks. "Breasts." She makes a half-hearted attempt to cover herself with her shirt.

Moving to the bed, I lean in to take a closer look at her shoulder. "It's not bleeding. You'll be OK. Go shower and put on something clean."

In the front room, I take a seat on the couch next to Bryer, whose cheeks have returned to a much cooler—and safer—aqua. Her voice is still harsh. "Dammit, Rix."

Across the room, Erlandr sits with his head in his hands. "I should never have gone out tonight, but Azul was hungry, and Matt and David were here, so ..."

"It's not your fault. It's mine," Bryer murmurs. She's full of surprises. "Ultimately *everything* that happens in this house is my responsibility."

"You can't call back the tide," I murmur, returning my focus to her. "How safe do you think the house is?"

Erlandr raises his head. "I was careful not to come straight here. No one followed us."

"At least someone kept his head," Bryer mutters. "The cops don't move very fast, particularly when it comes to the homeless, so we should have a few days. You"—she points at me—"are moving into Corvina's room." When I open my mouth to protest, she cuts me off. "No arguing. Erlandr can stay with her for now, so you can go pick up your things. But I expect you back here tomorrow night. For good."

My heart sinks. What will I tell Maggie? I check the time. "I need to go."

I don't get back to Maggie's until nearly five. After waiting to hear her slippers on the kitchen floor, I text her.

Good morning. Can I join you for coffee?

Sure. Come on up.

When I get to the kitchen, she's sitting at the island, sipping her coffee. Another cup waits for me. I slide onto the stool across from her. "How'd you sleep?"

"OK. Did you just get in?"

"Mm-hm. Something came up."

"In the middle of the night? Weren't you working?"

"I worked. I just had to go out."

"You seem a little ... distraught. Are you OK?" She nibbles her bagel.

"Just some business I need to take care of. I'll be away for a day or two, but maybe more."

"What about your new job? I thought that was taking all of your time."

"It is. I'll need to squeeze it in for a couple of days. I'm in a good position, though. I finished meeting all my new employees. Now I'm working on a quarterly plan. I don't need to be online so much to do that."

"Oh. Well, I'm planning to work an ER shift tonight." She bites into her bagel, chews, then swallows before continuing. "I'm napping this afternoon, as soon as I finish my last appointment at two. I won't see you, then." Even with her unkempt hair and tired eyes, I still love gazing at her. I smile. "What?" She breaks my trance.

"I'll miss you."

"You're acting very strange. Are you sure everything's all right?"

"It'll be all right." I sip my coffee. It's already cooling. "How are things in the ER?"

"Fairly frantic, most nights. The upward slope of positive cases is alarming, to say the least. When will we start to get things more under control? It's already worse than the initial wave. We just hit three million cases."

"And setting new records every day. Americans are stubborn. I doubt we'll make much headway until a vaccine's available."

"That looks promising, at least. Maybe by early next year."

"I hope it doesn't take that long. I worry about you."

"I've got you to take care of me." She smiles, and I get lost again in her eyes. "You'd do that, wouldn't you?"

"Um ..." I blink. How do I answer that? I don't even know if I'll be here. "As long as I'm in your home, I'll take care of you."

She slides off her stool. "Well, I'd better get ready." After putting her dishes in the sink, she leaves me to finish my coffee alone. I wash everything, then head downstairs.

My alarm wakes me at three. I login to my laptop and open the quarterly plan. Regardless of what Bryer said, I'm not taking all my things over there, although without my computer, my phone'll be my only workspace. An hour later, the upstairs shower starts. That was a quick nap. She's wearing herself out. I go back to my document.

A text alert from Maggie pops up.

> Gotta go. See you in a few. Stay safe.

The front door bumps closed. In the background, Dave Grohl softly sings 'Everlong.' Will I ever breathe her in again? I push down to still my bouncing knee. While I re-read the same paragraph for the third time, The Foo Fighters continue. Nothing will *ever* be this good again. I give up and close my computer.

After a quick shower, I throw all my dirty clothes in the washer, then scrub the bathroom, and vacuum my room and the hallway. As the laundry spins, I gather the sheets and towels, then start the next load. I work on the doc, this time with more success. By the time my clothes are dry, I'm halfway done.

Another text pops, this one from Nalini.

> How're you doing with your new team?

> Made it thru the initial interviews. Some are sad to no longer work directly for you, but they're excited about your promotion.

> You'll be fine. How's the plan coming?

> Working on it now. Rough draft
> complete. Will get it to you by early next
> week. My internet may be spotty for a
> day or two. Is it all right to have the team
> contact you if they need something
> immediately and can't get through
> to me?

> Sure sure. Only one day until the
> weekend. :-) Have a good one.

> You, too. Stay safe.

> Stay safe. TTYL

After texting my team, I tug on my oldest pair of jeans and a faded t-shirt. When I'm done folding and putting away the best of my clothing, I pull out my daypack, glad that I picked up this smaller one so I wouldn't need to carry my big one back and forth to Bryer's. I stuff in a couple of shirts, some underwear and socks, and my toothbrush, toothpaste and comb. Checking the time, I realize I'm running late. I text Maggie.

> My sheets and towels are in the dryer.
> Sorry to leave the work to you. Stay safe.

3

SHREDDED HEART

July 9 to 10, 2020
Rix

When I walk through the door, Bryer punches my shoulder. Her face glows soft tangerine, exposing her uncertainty, fear and anger. "What took you so long?" She peers at my pack. "And where's all your things?"

"I was working and ran out of time. I'll get the rest later."

With a nod toward Corvina's room, she says, "Stow your gear on your cot, and let's get going." She meets my eyes. "We're paired for tonight."

This should be interesting. I've never hunted alone with Bryer before. The night would be pleasant, if not for the circumstances. We take a circuitous route to Green Lake.

"Thanks for not abandoning me," she murmurs. "I wasn't sure if you'd show up."

"I'm not a jerk."

"According to who?" Her cheeks cool to faint aqua. "I need someone like you to help me hold things together. Cleve's too soft."

Am I not also soft? "He's gentle. That's not a bad thing." When she doesn't comment, I ask, "What do you need?"

"Just trying to make some decisions. Only a few of us will fit at the house in Shoreline. They already don't have enough beds. I don't know how to choose." She shakes her head, causing her fuchsia moussed hair to sway. "And the short nights will make it hard to get there, especially carrying our stuff."

"This time of year it's difficult to do anything."

"I'll send Matt and David. Matt will need to find a new job. And maybe David will finally get one. But they'll do OK there." Her voice is resigned. "Azul's good on her own. And Erlandr can go with her. I don't know what to do with that kid. She's got a proven track record, now. We can't trust her."

"Guarding her every night isn't practical."

"We should just throw her out."

I stare at her. "Seriously? She won't last for long. And she may end up killing someone who's not already dead."

"Oh, I mean throw her outside. Midday."

This is a side of Bryer I didn't expect. "You'll need to do that when Erlandr's not around." I take a shaky breath. "And me." I need to find a safe place to move them, at least until Bryer cools down. But I understand her reaction. Children make terrible vampires.

"I can arrange that." She picks up her pace. "We may

as well get our fill. Who knows when we'll be able to hunt again."

Along the west side of the lake, she selects our first victim. Before he strides past the little theater, she leads me into a clump of trees further up the lake. "Stay here. I'll be right back."

While she's gone, I carefully search the growing shadows in the shrubs surrounding the tiny grove for hidden campers. She returns with a sweaty, muscular man a little taller than me and leads him behind one of the trees. I stand watch for a few minutes until she softly calls, "Rix." After another quick look around, I duck into the bushes. The smell of blood draws me. My fangs spring to life. "Quick." Bryer's lips gleam crimson, contrasting with the bright white of her still-protruding fangs. "Before it healsth."

"Wipe your mouth," I whisper, handing her a packet.

As I drop onto the man's neck, she moves away to take over guard duty. "Remember. He's just the appetizer," she murmurs.

When I stop and hold my hand to the man's neck, Bryer appears beside me. She presses her mouth against mine and uses her tongue to lick the remnants of blood from my lips. "Mmm. Sweet."

Frowning at her, I pull out a hand wipe and swab off the man's neck. "You need to be more careful in the dark."

Bryer pats his shoulder. "On your way."

With a confused expression, he waves and dashes up to the trail.

As I wipe my hands on the still-damp cloth, Bryer nods. "Those are such a good idea."

Bryer and I walk south along the narrow stretch of trail between the lake and Aurora Avenue until we can head up into Woodland Park. "Sorry about that, back there." Her cheeks shimmer like a ruby. "I forgot it was you, and not Cleve. The blood makes me a little crazy."

"It *was* a surprise. How long have you known him?"

"A couple of years. He was green, so I adopted him. Showed him the ropes. It's been safer, having a partner. We should find you one."

"I've never been good with relationships. No offense, but I feel safer alone."

"You're a man. That helps."

"I never really thought about the challenges of being a woman vampire. I guess they're similar to any woman."

"Oh, no. There's no comparison. I was never completely safe outside my home or work. And not always there. No woman is. Especially at night. Even though I worked out and lifted weights, I still couldn't protect myself from being transitioned. It's ironic. I've never been as safe as I am now." Stopping, she turns to me. "I have real power."

"How long have you ..." my voice trails off.

"A long time. You?"

"World War Two."

"Oh, *that's* a long time," she murmurs. "I heard rumors about the Nazis trying to raise a demon army."

"I'm proof they're true."

Forcing a smile, she touches my shoulder. "Let's keep hunting or we'll need to quit before we're full."

We feed off and on until very late—or very early. Even with the virus and it being Thursday, folks are walking around the lake and, to a lesser degree, in the park.

Bryer relaxes as she talks—even if I share very little—finally telling me her transition story. "I was on my way to my car after working late. No one else was around. A man grabbed me and dragged me behind some dumpsters at a construction site." She glances over at me. "That's where it happened."

"You must have felt helpless."

"I was. He was a vampire." She snorts a laugh. "But he wasn't very good at it."

"What do you mean?"

"He took too much. I would've died, so he ..." She shrugs. "You know." When I nod, she adds, "He also fed me way more of his blood than I needed to survive, so that might have weakened him, but it helped me recover quickly. I was so mad, I fought him. And I was stronger than I had ever been. Probably stronger than he was. I threw his ass into one of the bins, but it was full of wood scraps. He landed on a sharp piece." Mixed emotions swirl across her face. "And that was that."

"It wasn't your fault."

"No. It was his." She checks the sky. "We have time for dessert and then we should head back. Your turn to choose."

When I return a few minutes later with a blonde twenty-something clutching my arm, Bryer's brows rise. I shrug and lead my victim past her, behind a pair of big firs. The young woman giggles when I touch her neck. I've never fed on a ticklish person before. "Shh." I hold my fingers to her lips, which prompts her to kiss them.

Turning her head away, I press my fangs deep into her neck. The iron-rich liquid is tainted with something I don't recognize. She must have been out partying all night. I only feed for a short while, then whisper, "Your turn." Bryer quickly takes my place. "She may be on drugs," I mutter before moving away to stand guard.

A couple walking against the one-way traffic on the main trail resolves into cops. As they pass the early morning exercisers, one holds out a piece of paper. A walker stops to chat with them while studying it. He points toward the woods, then moves on. When they spot me, they veer in my direction. Looping my mask behind my ears, I stroll down to the path, diverting them away from Bryer.

They slow, blocking my way. "Excuse me, sir." I stop, thankful for the six foot rule. The woman holds up a rough sketch of a teenaged girl who looks a lot like Corvina. "Have you seen this girl?"

Leaning in for effect, I study the image. I shrug. "What did she do?"

She turns it over to show me a second image. "How about this boy?" Crude, but Erlandr. Of course. I purse my brow and stare intently. When I reach for it, she snatches it away. "If you see either of them, call nine one one." She folds the paper and slips it into her pocket. "Be careful out here alone."

I nod and step past, walking very slowly, then stop and watch until they're out of sight around the Aqua Theater. As a briskly walking couple nears, I pick out snatches of their mask-muted conversation: "... can you believe ..."; "... it's horrible ..."; "... only fifteen ..."; "... maybe an animal attack ...”; “... I heard a *vampire* ...”; “... silly—they’re not real ... .” Their nervous laughter doesn’t mask their unease. I hurry back to Bryer’s tree.

As we head toward the house, I whisper, “The cops were showing pictures of Corvina and Erlandr to people.”

“Shit,” she mutters. “I thought we’d have more time. I told you that kid’s trouble.”

July 10, 2020
Rix

A pale rose paints the northeastern horizon as we turn onto Forty-ninth. Flashing blue lights near 99 halt our quiet conversation. At the corner of Whitman, we duck behind a hedge to peer up the street.

“I hope that’s at the apartments next door,” Bryer whispers.

When I spot a big black van and several riot clad ... police? ..., I pull her back toward Whitman. “We need to get out of here.”

“What’s going on?”

“It’s an abduction. Like the one at the apartment I shared with Robert last fall. He got away, but DB wasn’t as lucky.” I tug on her arm. “Come on. The sun’ll be up soon.”

“No.”

“Keep your voice down.”

“I can’t leave Cleve.”

“You don’t even know if he’s there.” I hold her eyes.

"There's nothing you can do if he is." Slinging my arm around her shoulders, I pull her along with me. "Let's see if we can find a vantage point a little closer."

Even though all my instincts tell me to run, I keep our pace on the quick side of normal. Once we turn the corner onto North Forty-eighth, we dash to the last house before the highway and duck into its narrow side yard. At the fence, we slip behind the small shed and raise our noses high enough to see into the next yard. Although growing daylight illuminates the bushes, we aren't close enough to see across the street to Bryer's house. We scurry over the fence. Scuttling to the end of the house, cloaked behind a large rhody, we watch with wide eyes as the scene across the street unfolds.

"Let me go!" David's voice rises above other, more muted shouts and cries coming from inside. "What did I do?" In the doorway, he appears, struggling to break free from the men holding his arms, but his wrists are zip tied behind him. Even with the strength of a vampire, he's no match for them.

Standing off to the side, a man in a brown leather jacket watches. "Shut him up," he says, almost casually.

Another man snugs a black bag over David's head, making his words too muffled to understand. The two holding his arms toss him into the back of the van.

Next, Azul appears, barefooted, with naked legs emerging from a baggy t-shirt. She saunters between two men holding her arms. Her calm demeanor belies the telltale fiery blush to her cheeks. When she licks one man's neck, he twists away to avoid the contact. She slips from his clutches. Jabbing her elbow into the other man's ribs, she nearly breaks free. She hesitates, takes a quick look at the sky. The first recovers his balance, and two more tackle her from behind.

"Why isn't it zip tied?" The man in the jacket asks, this time a little louder. A blush of fearful tangerine uncertainty touches his cheeks.

Even though she no longer resists, one kneels—full weight—on her neck and head, with another straddling her hips. A third pins down her ankles while the fourth slips zip ties around her wrists, binding them behind her back. After he cinches a bag over her head, she's jerked to her feet and hurled into the van.

My anxiety rises with the approaching sun, which casts an amber glow on the steadily brightening world, forcing me to squint and blink. We're no longer safe out here. From inside the house, Corvina's clearly audible screams rivet me. Two burly men, twice her size, drag the girl, kicking and snarling, from the house. On one man's cheek, two parallel scratches ooze bright red blood. The angry scarlet glow from Corvina's cheeks extends down her neck, competing with the radiance of the coming sun. Her naked body reveals how very thin she is. Even in the shade of the doorway and from this distance, the gleam of her fangs is visible as she tries to bite the men restraining her arms. With a loud crack, another man punches her in the jaw. I cover my mouth so I don't cry out. With her toes barely touching the ground, she hangs limply by her arms.

Two more men emerge onto the porch with Erlandr between them, wearing only his boxers. A trickle of blood runs from a cut near his eye—probably from trying to protect Corvina—but one of the men sports a quickly swelling lip. Walking calmly between them, with no heat in his cheeks, he seems resigned to his fate. His lips move, as if whispering a prayer. For a fleeting moment, he looks in my direction. A faint smile makes me think he knows I'm here.

Stinging tears blur my vision. I feel so helpless. They're my responsibility, but there's nothing I can do to help. "We should go," I whisper into Bryer's ear. We can no longer make it to Maggie's. Maybe the park?

"Not yet. I haven't seen Cleve."

As my two young friends are dragged from the shadow of the house into the bright morning sun, first Corvina, then Erlandr, burst into flame. I gasp, surprised by how quickly they burn. One moment, they're standing there, plain as day. The next, they just disappear. How painful is that? No one but me will even care that they're gone. The men who hold them show no surprise. They wait to let go until the last possible second, then watch as the ashes swirl around their feet, dusting their shiny black boots in a soft, grey coat. One smirks. "Oops."

The man giving orders grunts, "Dammit. We're supposed to bring them in."

"We've got two. No one will care about these others."

The brightness of the sunlight hurts my eyes, even with them squeezed to tiny slits. "We need to go. Now."

"No no no no," Bryer moans. When I clamp my hand over her mouth, she bites deep into the skin between my thumb and forefinger. Despite the pain, my grip remains firm. With my other arm wrapped around her waist, I haul her to the backyard. Letting go of her mouth, I hoist her up onto the fence. She lingers at the top, still searching for Cleve.

Beyond the shadow cast by the roof of the house, sunlight bathes the top of the shed. Leaving is no longer a possibility. We need to find somewhere to hide. "Keep moving," I frantically whisper. When Bryer drops to the other side, I vault over right behind her. She's hunched in the corner between the shed and the fence, with her head in her hands. "Maybe we can stay inside this shed," I say softly, although she makes no indication she heard. "I'm not certain there will be enough shade for both of us back there." I try the latch. The door swings open. Grabbing Bryer's sleeve, I heave her inside, then squeeze in and pull the door shut. With barely enough room to put our feet among the tools and gear, it's going to be a long, long day.

Voices from the next street drift into the tiny building.

"Here's another one."

"Jesus! It almost burned me."

Bryer whimpers. I hold her closer. Her body shakes with her tears.

July 10 to 11, 2020
Rix

Both Bryer and I text Cleve and Matt, but neither responds. Thankfully, no one comes to the shed during the day. Leaning against me, with my arms around her, Bryer sleeps through a lot of it. Late in the afternoon, she opens her eyes, and murmurs, "Dammit, Rix. What do we do now?"

"Find a safe place to pull ourselves together." Tilting my head back, I look into her eyes. "And start over."

"You've been through this before."

"Not this. I don't know *what* this is." I wiggle my feet, trying to get rid of the tingling from standing so long in one spot. "But I have left on a moment's notice. More than once. It's inevitable, if you intend to survive."

"I don't know if I want to"—she stifles a sob—"without Cleve."

This is one of the reasons I don't get into relationships. "Maybe he was able to hide." Snugging her close, I rub her back. "Maybe he hadn't returned yet."

"Maybe."

"I'll bet his phone is dead." I give her a little smile, but she only drops her head to my shoulder. "Let's head up to the Hill and see if we can find a safe place to stay. Maybe with ... Robert." I do *not* want to stay with him, but with no other option, I will. "I want to check on some of the folks up there. Try to warn them."

"I'm going to Shoreline. They need to be warned, too. If Cleve made it, he'll go there." She tugs on my sleeve. "Come with me."

"I'll come find you later. I need to do this first."

Waiting until the summer sun strolls over the horizon, well after nine, we slip out and onto the street. At the corner, I kiss Bryer's cheek. "Good hunting, my friend."

After a hug, she turns and trudges away.

At nearly eleven, I arrive at Darah's and knock on the door. A moment later, the porch light turns off. I must not be welcome. As I start to turn, the door opens wide enough for Darah's face to appear. She reaches out to grab my jacket and tugs me. I step inside. After quickly shutting the door, she hisses, "What are you doing here?"

"Looking for James. What happened?"

Her eyes drop and dart from side to side. "He's gone."

My gut fills with dread. "What do you mean, gone?"

"Some men ... cops or soldiers or something ..." She meets my gaze. "They took him. And a couple of his friends."

"When?"

"Two nights ago." She peers out the peephole. "You should leave."

"Are you involved in this?"

"I ..." She rolls her back to the wall. Her lower lip trembles. Her eyes stay locked on the floor.

I stand with my body nearly touching hers and lightly press two fingers to her chin to pull her head up. "What did you do?"

"I had a party. It got pretty wild." Tears fill her eyes. "It's my fault."

"It's not your fault, Darah." I drop my hand to her shoulder. "Take a breath, and tell me what happened."

"It *is* my fault." The tears spill down her cheeks. One lands on my hand, burning like a cinder. I wipe it away on my jeans. She rubs a hand across her face. "I've been telling some of my friends about James and the others—trying to get them to join me. The party was Robert's idea, though."

"See. I told you it's not your fault."

She nods, sniffs. "One of my friends from work came,

but she brought her boyfriend and he was some kind of cop, and not much later, a bunch more cops showed up." She takes a breath and scrunches her face. "They weren't like any cops I'd ever seen, all dressed in black riot gear, like a SWAT team? But they didn't have badges, or any markings at all—like 'police'—on their gear." Drawing another breath, she goes on in a rush, words overflowing like the spillway at the Locks. "And they carried wooden clubs with sharp ends, like short spears. And, um, maybe cattle prods? And they took away all the vampires, and told everyone else we were breaking social distancing guidelines and to go home." She puts her hand on my chest and pushes lightly. "You should get out of here, John. They may still be watching me. Go out the rear."

After long detours to ensure no one's tailing me, it takes the rest of the night to get back to Maggie's. Did I draw those men here? Oh my gods. Am I the connection between the two raids? And the one last winter? Are they after *me*? I thought I was beyond all that. They haven't caught up with me since the fifties. It's definitely time to move on. I absolutely do *not* want Maggie to be involved in this.

When I cross the Fremont Bridge, I glance at my phone for the time. Five-fifteen? Already? I may have pushed it too far. The sky's so bright I avert my eyes from the northeastern horizon. Still, running could draw attention to myself, since I'm not dressed for an early morning jog. I stride up the hill and try to look confident—like I belong here—but can't help glancing behind me every few steps.

As I turn onto Maggie's street, sunlight paints the rooftops. Before I can cross, it creeps down the sides of the houses and bathes the center of the road. Stepping into the shadows of the house across from hers, I watch the last of the shade disappear from her yard. Maggie comes onto the porch, and looks up and down the street. She must have just gotten home. Doesn't she ever sleep? Worry creases her forehead. My eyes linger on her, squinting more and more, until she goes back inside. Without another option, I dash past the neighbor's house to their backyard.

July 10 to 11, 2020
Maggie

With Rix gone again, the quiet house feels empty —like after Dad died. I hope nothing's seriously wrong, but he was acting so strangely. I'm tired, but feel weirdly relieved when Althea asks me to work again tonight. A late shift this time—nine to three. Ugh. Friday nights are always so busy, and the ER never fails to live up to its reputation as 'the zoo.' I'll wait to eat until I get there and see if anything's left.

Rama greets me with smiling eyes when I arrive at the nurses' station. He always has a smile for me. "Working again? When's the last time you had a night off?"

"You sound just like ..." My eyes pinch, along with my diaphragm. "Tomorrow's Saturday. I can rest then."

He studies me. "Is everything all right between you and Rix?"

How does he read me so easily? My shoulders rise and fall with my breath. "I think so. When's the last time *you* had a day off?"

"Hmm."

"See? None of us will rest until we're beyond this pandemic."

"I can't believe the US is averaging fifty-four thousand a day. I wonder how long *this* wave will go on."

I frown. "We're well beyond the peak of the first wave here."

"Fifty percent higher." Somehow Rama produces another eye-crinkling smile. "It's good the CDC recognized it's likely airborne. That should help prevent large gatherings."

"And maybe convince more folks to wear masks." I stretch. "Let's hope it's slow tonight."

As soon as I utter the words, we get notified of an approaching aid car. I watch as the man is wheeled in. Blood soaks through a large gauze pad on his shin, exposed where the leg of his pants was cut open. The triage is quick. I follow as Rama guides the gurney to a room. The man tears off his mask and hurls it at him. "I'm not wearing this fucking mask," he fumes, spittle spraying on Rama's plastic shield. "I can't breathe. And they ruined my best fucking pair of jeans."

Rama remains completely composed. "Let's get you into the room so we can take a look at your leg." Isolating him is definitely preferable to the risk of exposing everyone in the hallway. I pull the curtain shut. Not forcing the mask issue was a good move. The man's noticeably calmer. At the computer, Rama logs in. "I need to confirm some information before we get started. What's your name?" As the man recites his name and birthdate, he calms further. "Since we're so confined in here, will you wear a mask?" Rama holds one out. "I don't want you to contract COVID on top of all this." The man surprises me by taking it.

As Rama fits the BP cuff around the man's arm, I move to the bloody leg. "Let's see what you've got going on here."

An hour later, we both scrub. I shake my head. "Wow."

Rama carefully cleans his face shield before donning new gloves. "I'm so glad these were donated to us. We're lucky to have such solid support from local businesses."

"Does *anything* phase you?" I can't believe he's so blasé about what just happened. "The spit could almost be defined as assault."

"I find that if I can remain calm, everything goes more smoothly." He looks at me thoughtfully. "It wasn't intentional. Would you really have him charged with a felony?"

"No. You're right." I sigh. "You did the right thing by not forcing him to follow the rules. I wouldn't have given in so easily." I walk beside him back to the nurses' station. "I learn from you every time we work together."

He beams in the praise. "I'll take that compliment."

"I'm really glad you're my friend." I hope he can see my smile behind my mask. "What time's dinner?"

"Soon. I shifted my break to line up with yours."

We get called off to separate cases. Over the next couple of hours, we meet up only briefly a few times at the nurses' station. When there's a lull, Rama tugs my sleeve. "It's time. Let's eat."

The aroma of pizza beckons us well before the row of boxes comes into view. Several large containers of Caesar salad await us at the end of the long table. With our plates piled high, we sit to eat.

"Feels good to get off my feet for a moment." Rama folds his pizza, something he learned while living in New York City with his aunt, and takes a bite. "This is excellent pizza. I'm glad it's still hot. My aunt would approve." His eyes pinch in pain.

"She was such a nice person. I'm glad I got to meet her when she came to visit. I didn't know she knew Althea until then." I poke a forkful of salad—crispy, lightly dressed, amply covered in shaved parmesan—and get it to my mouth before the lettuce slips off the plastic fork. "Mmm. Good."

"Taraji was a good person. I'm truly blessed. It was through her friendship with Althea that I found out about this position. They were friends since since their college days." The sun returns to his smile. "Have the pizza while it's still hot." He pops in the last bite and starts on his second slice.

We quickly eat the remainder in silence. As we walk back to the nurses' station, Rama watches me. When I don't fill the conversational void, he finally asks, "What's going on with Rix?"

I meet his eyes. Blink. Purse my brow. "He moved out again."

"Did you ask him to leave?"

"No." I shake my head vehemently.

"For how long?"

"He said a day or two. Something about handling some business." I temper the sarcasm in my voice. "It's been two days, and I haven't heard a peep from him."

"All you can do is be patient. He'll return to you in his own time."

"I hope you're right."

We hardly see each other until three, when I'm heading out. "Rama," I call, as he's dashing off to another emergency. "I'm done. See you next time."

"Stay safe, Maggie."

When I arrive home to my dark house, I suck in my lower lip to keep it from trembling. Rix isn't here. After decontaminating and bathing, I go out onto the porch. The sun's already rising. I guess there's no chance of him coming home today.

I clomp up the stairs and crawl wearily into bed. Before turning off the light, I finally open my phone. Disappointment tears at my heart when I find no messages from Rix. I text him.

> Where are you? Is everything going OK? Did you get settled in somewhere? Are you safe? I'm worried about you. Going to sleep now. Dreaming of you.

I hit send and set the phone on the nightstand. Despite the sunlight making its way into my room, I can't keep my eyes open any longer. Snugging against my pillow, I whisper, "Goodnight, Rix."

July 11, 2020
Rix

After surveying my surroundings, my anxiety mounts. The sun will be tough to avoid all day without being seen. Tucked in the back of the yard, near an impressively tall fence at least my height, is a garden shed. Enough shade covers the yard for me to scurry across and try the latch. It's locked. I squeeze between the shed and the fence. Good thing I'm so small. I doubt Cleve or Matt would fit. If they're still around. Stay focused, Rix. The corner is my best option for shade, as long as the fence boards have a tight enough fit. The tall weeds should help keep me hidden. With my back to the fence, I huddle with my knees drawn up to my chin. Maybe I can sleep like this for a while. I'll be surprised to make it to sunset.

Before closing my eyes, I remember a waiting text. I fish the phone from my pocket and turn it on. After two days, I'm lucky it still has a quarter of a battery. I'll need to be frugal until I can find a way to charge it. Thumbing it open, I expect to find a text from Nalini. My heart catches when I see a notification on Signal. It's from Maggie. *Where are you? Is everything going OK? Did you g...* is all I can read. I don't open it. I don't want her to know I've seen it. Or that I'm still nearby. After switching the phone to airplane mode, I shut it down and shove it into my pocket. When I wedge myself into the corner, to lean against both the back and side fences, her window comes into view.

The light is on and the shade is open, but I can only make out her silhouette. And then, she's gone.

I sleep in snatches, too worried about the sun to ignore it for long. Mostly, I'm bored. And my rear hurts from sitting on the rocky ground. I shift, check the position of the sun, and try to sleep. Something tickles my cheek. I swat at it, then come fully awake to watch a big brown hairy spider dash away down my arm. I rise to a crouch and brush myself off. Even though they don't bite vampires, I can't stand anything crawling on me.

Shifting to sit against the side fence, I stretch my legs along the back one. This is the most dangerous time of day. The midday sun is so high in the sky, I have only a narrow triangle of shade. When it reaches its zenith, I'm forced to lie down for a while. I try hard not to drift off to sleep, but maybe that would be better.

As the sun slowly creeps to the northwest, shadows extend across most of the yard. The scrape and clang of a barbecue being dragged onto a concrete porch startle me awake. I must have drifted off. Uncertain if it's in this yard or the next, I get to my feet, in case I need to duck from sight. It actually feels good to stand. Soon, the odor of grilled meat wafts to my corner. The clink of silverware and plates and glasses tells me dinner will be served outside. I make out the voices of a man and a woman chatting softly as they eat, and remember dinner conversations with my wife—a lot of the same conversations I've had with Maggie, full of talk about medicine, economics, and the fear of fascism. I try to stay completely silent, but shift slightly from foot to foot, causing the occasional grind of rock on rock, but too soft for them to hear. I remain highly alert until the dishes are cleared and the voices fade into the house.

A dog in the next yard must have picked up my scent when it was let out to relieve itself. It stands no more than several inches away—thankfully, on the other side of the fence—barking and snarling. "Howie! Get in here." It gives me two more half-hearted growls before obeying its master.

I'm so ready for the sun to be gone. Edging my way to the corner of the shed, I peek into the yard. No direct light, so it must be around nine. I scuttle along the fence until it ends abruptly, about even with the front of the house. It's a good spot to wait for the golden streaks of setting sun to fade from Maggie's yard.

July 11 to 12, 2020
Rix

As the last rays of sun disappear, I steal across the street, hoping the flat light conceals my passage. The lamps in Maggie's living room are on, so she must be home. She really should put her lights on timers, so passersby don't know she isn't home in the evenings. Dashing along the house, I slip into the backyard and duck into her little garden sanctuary in the far corner. Deep in the shadows, the burbling fountain drowns out the city noise that the soft, moss covered ground doesn't muffle. I sit to gather my thoughts, and the tension leaves my shoulders.

Using my hoodie to shield the light, I turn on my phone and dim it as low as it will go. Can I risk checking my messages? After turning off airplane mode, I resist the urge to open a new message from Maggie. Instead, I text Nalini.

> Sorry for the late notice. Family emergency came up. Need to take a few days off.

Maybe only a few days. I hit send, switch back to airplane mode and power down the phone, as much to conserve its dwindling battery as to avoid being noticed. I see no way to circumvent the risk of entering the basement to grab my laptop and chargers, but need to wait until Maggie's asleep.

The light in the kitchen comes on. I catch sight of her at the sink, where only a couple of weeks ago she said, 'Some souls are destined to be together.' Scooting to where I can see more clearly, I hungrily try to catch another glimpse of her, however brief. When the outside light comes on, I scramble to the shadows under a big rhody. I pull my hood up and sit with my knees drawn to my chest. After dumping the kitchen waste into the compost bin in the other corner of the yard, Maggie strolls around, admiring her plants. Entering the mossy recess, she stops beside the fountain. I sit as still as a stalked mouse.

"I miss you so much, Dad. I wish you were still here." Her soft voice barely rises above the burble of the tiny cascade. She squats to poke her fingertips into the stream. "There's this guy, Rix, who lives in my basement. I don't know what to make of him. He seems to like me—he once said he loves me—but I think he's slipping away, and I don't know how to stop it." She draws in a deep breath and exhales audibly, fluttering her lips. My resolve to leave wavers. When she stands and shakes the water from her fingers, a few drops land on my cheek. I catch myself before I flinch. She wipes her hands on her pants. "He makes me feel … special, and I want very much not to lose that." Turning, she heads back into the house.

I really wish I hadn't witnessed that. I feel like a scoundrel for eavesdropping on something so personal. Moving from the shelter of the rhody to where I can watch the house, I wait. A short time later, the lights go off on the main floor. Maggie takes her time getting ready for bed, probably showering first. Finally, the house is dark. I wait some more, to allow her to fall asleep.

Slinking in the shadows along the fence, I go to the side door and carefully open it. Still, the deadbolt produces a loud click. When I'm inside, I stop to listen to the quiet house. The rumble of a passing truck causes a window to rattle. No other sounds come from inside. I creep down the half-stairway and the hallway to my room. I don't risk turning on a light. My night vision allows me to see well enough. After stripping, I pull on clean boxers, jeans, two t-shirts—less to pack—and my hoodie. I grab my backpack and slip my laptop into its sleeve, really glad now that I left most of my things here, and roll my remaining clothing into soft bricks to stack in the main compartment. From the bathroom, I retrieve my toilet kit. With some effort, I press it down onto my clothing enough to get the zipper to close. As I fuss with the new velcro straps I got to attach the inflatable mattress, a footfall on the stairs freezes me.

The clack of a key in the lock of the hallway door confirms Maggie's approach. As I slip my backpack to the rug against the bed, she softly calls, "Rix? Is that you?" The hall light comes on, leaking under the door.

I debate keeping my silence, but know how persistent Maggie can be. And I certainly don't want to frighten her. "I'm here."

"Is everything all right?"

"Just putting some things away."

"Are you sure everything's OK? I've been worried."

I can't do this. After flipping on the lamp, I open the door. "Come on in. Let's talk."

As she perches on the edge of the bed, her eyes lock on the overstuffed backpack. "What's going on?" Sitting on the bed between her and the pack, I break her focus. She raises her eyes to meet mine, and I swim in the dark pools until her brow furrows above them. "Talk to me."

"Something came up." I frown and look away. "I need to leave town unexpectedly."

"And you weren't going to tell me?"

"I couldn't bear to see you cry." I meet her gaze. The emotions on her face flit between anger, confusion and hurt. "I was going to leave a note." Am I reduced to whimpering? Her expression locks on hurt. "I'm sorry." The warmth of her hand under mine surprises me. When did I move my hand? "I'm really, really sorry," I whisper.

"Why are you leaving?" She switches to resolute. I can't restrain a little smile. "Don't try charming me. Answer the question."

Withdrawing my hand, I look down. "You remember James?"

"The guy you were rooming with? The one who runs with a bad crowd?" The volume of her voice rises with each question. "The one who stole from you? That James?"

"That James." I meet her eyes. "That crowd. They got into some really illegal things. Sexual things. They got busted."

"But, you didn't. Right?"

"Not exactly, but the house where I stayed when you kicked"—my voice catches—"when I moved out, they got raided, too." I blink back tears. "Bryer and I were out together. We were late getting back, or I would've been there. We watched from across the street."

"But, you didn't do anything wrong. Tell the authorities. They won't have anything to hold you on."

"It's more complicated than that. It was a vampire roundup. Two of them were taken away, and two more, probably three, didn't make it from the house to the van." My lungs won't expand.

"What does *that* mean?" Her eyes flit around as she thinks. She gasps. "Was the sun up?" I can only nod. "Does it work like"—she makes a little shrug—"on TV?"

"It does," I whisper.

"You mean they killed them?" She draws in a deep breath, prompting one in me. "How could they do that?"

"We have no legal status, as a person. We're not people. Look, I can't afford for them to find me." I don't *ever* want to go through that again. I'm so sorry Azul and David will. My knee jiggles. Maggie's hand stops it. I put mine over hers. "I need to go away—now—so no connection is made to you. You're the most important thing."

"Where will you go?" She sounds like a frightened child, small and weak. I think she may cry, and hope she doesn't. I don't know if I can leave her if she does.

"I haven't figured that out yet." I grimace. "I'll find a new place to start over. It's not the first time. It won't be the last." I peer at Maggie. She looks so sad. "It is the first time I'm leaving someone behind. I'm sorry I let you get involved with me."

"Please don't go," she whispers.

"I wish it didn't have to end this way, but really ... it's for the best." I gently cup her cheek, then let my hand drop. "Find yourself a normal man to love, someone you can make a family with and grow old with. That's not me. That could never be me."

Flames bloom on her neck. Her voice is loud and harsh. "Why don't I get a say in this?" She shakes her head, then asks softly, "When will I see you again?"

"I don't know."

"I love you." She squeezes the tears from her eyes—and pouts. Beautiful even when she pouts.

"I'm sorry." My shredded heart is bleeding. "Please leave me with a smile, Maggie May."

4

LOST

July 12, 2020
Rix

I'm without housing. Again. My highest priority is to find a place for the day. And soon. The sun will rise in a couple of hours. The summer nights in Seattle are far too short. No hope of making my way up to Shoreline to try to find Bryer. I should text her soon, but not tonight. I slink from the yard and head down the street.

Staying off the arterials, I roughly parallel Thirty-ninth toward the U-District, to put some distance between me and Woodland Park. The College Inn has rooms with a single bed for fifty-nine dollars, but I spend the extra twenty-five a night to get a private bath. The cash in my wallet should last a few days, enough time to move assets, acquire new IDs, get a new simcard and create accounts. I need to get out of this city, but those come first.

The new day is nearly upon me as I shut the door to

the room. Heaving my bag onto the bed, I unzip it, pull out my laptop and plug it in. How did it get down to two percent? My phone needs a new chip, but I need new credentials first. I insert the power cord. Pulling out my clothing, I put the socks and underwear in the dresser, and hang the shirts and jeans so they don't get too wrinkled. Not much left. I'll be forced to do a load of laundry before I leave. At least, everything fits in my pack now.

Since I haven't bathed in two long, very rough days, I strip and turn on the shower. By the time I finish, the dawn sky glows brightly. After carefully closing the curtains, ensuring no gaps will let in the sun, I slip between the crisp sheets. How safe will I be here? I'm surprised I made it this long.

I try to sleep, but every little noise has me peering around. Without devices, or even a book to read, I lie rigidly on my back with my eyes closed. And see Maggie: the smooth curve of her jaw; her smile, full lips frosted with powdered sugar from the almond croissants she's so fond of; tears brimming on eyes that have enchanted me far too many times, dark jewels that beg me to stay.

Opening my computer, I check the battery. Good enough for some music. Maybe that will help me fall asleep. After choosing an easy-listening playlist and turning the volume down to its lowest audible level, I drop to my pillow. I'm so tired, my eyelids close of their own volition. I drift into that dreamy state between wakefulness and sleep. The ethereal guitar riff of Chris Isaak's 'Wicked Game' floats in rising and falling glissandos. The words begin. At first, they elude me, but then I hear each one. In my wildest dreams, I never imagined I would meet

Maggie. I can no longer breathe. My hand gropes for the lid and closes it, cutting off the chorus. Why did I let myself fall in love?

Salty liquid stings my eyes. I squeeze the lids tight, but it doesn't help. Pools form in my ears, then drizzle down my neck. Flopping to my side, I embrace the pillow. And begin to sob. It wasn't supposed to end this way: leaving the person I love; losing most of the folks I know; on the run again. The boat I so carefully navigated through this storm capsized, and I'm trapped inside with no way out until another big wave tosses her upright—if she doesn't sink first. My weeping turns to whimpering gasps, then deep ragged breaths.

I don't remember falling asleep, but my body jerks me awake. Since the world that leaks in past the window blind is still quite blinding, I roll over and cover my head with the blanket. In the muffled darkness, my mind lets go.

July 12, 2020
Rix

When the daylight fades, I set out for Ravenna Park. Green Lake's too risky. I want to get in one more feeding before I hit the road. Who knows when I'll be able to again. I turn up The Ave. The Target is still open. Maybe my luck's changing. I loop my mask behind my ears and go in to purchase a new SIM card. That's a major step forward. I continue north.

At the bus stop outside Costas Greek Restaurant, I approach someone bent over the sidewalk garbage can, holding an open yogurt container upright with one hand while digging through the trash with the other. He stands —just a kid—letting the lid drop shut, and stares at a piece of paper he pulled out. The police sketch of Corvina. The boy's head jerks toward me, and he nearly takes off.

"Hold on." Slipping my mask off one ear, I attempt a winning smile. "Did you know her?"

He shrugs. "Looks like Corvina, a girl I knew a few months ago."

"That's her. What do you know about her?"

He eyes me suspiciously. "Who wants to know?"

"Just a friend." I hate to use food as a bribe for someone I know is hungry, but I don't have time to gain his confidence without it. "If you tell me what you know about her"—I glance around for a fast-food joint—"I'll buy you a burger."

His tongue peeks out to wet his lips. He looks at the picture. "There's a Jack in the Box down here."

As he turns, the paper flutters to the ground. I snatch it. Pulling out my phone, I look up the site. "They're only doing curbside pickup. You'll need to order online." I hand the phone to him and follow as he orders. When I turn the paper over, Erlandr stares back at me. I fold it, then slip it into my pocket.

The youth twists his head to ask, "Can I have a shake, too?"

"Sure." I nod. "Get whatever you want." He hands me my phone and takes a bite of yogurt using the spoon that was in the container. How long until he contracts COVID? I input my cash card number before remembering I wasn't going to use it, in case they can trace it back to my new number. Like so many things recently, it's beyond my control now. I pocket the phone. "It'll be about five minutes."

"Didn't you order anything?"

"I don't eat fast food. What's your name?"

"Jaw"—he points to his cheek—"Knee"—he moves his finger to his knee—"Boy"—he taps his chest. When he repeats it at normal speed, it sounds like Johnny Boy.

I smile. "Clever."

"How come you're not afraid of gettin' the virus from me?" He peers at me.

"I'm probably immune." I'm always surprised by how easily youths will take the word of an adult. When the restaurant worker brings out the food, Jaw Knee Boy grabs it and immediately opens the bag. "Let's go over to the park." I indicate across the street. "We can talk while you eat."

Crossing Fiftieth, we head into the grassy area beyond the sidewalk. Before I get myself seated, he's already three bites into the burger. "This is good. I'm tired of eatin' other people's garbage."

"Where will you stay tonight? Do you have someplace safe?"

He shrugs and shoves a whole onion ring into his mouth. As he chews, he points vaguely to the east. "There's a shelter that usually has a bed. They been harder to find, since the virus." He takes a gulp of the milkshake. "At least the weather's been mostly dry."

As much as I want to, this boy is another child I can't help. I can't even help myself right now. "Where'd you meet Corvina?"

"We both stayed at the PSKS shelter—they're closed now—back in the before." When I raise my brows, he clarifies, "Before COVID." Maybe shortly before I met her. He picks up his burger, but doesn't take a bite before setting it down again. "She got kicked out or just ran, like all of us. Doesn't really matter. After they tried to send her home, she quit doin' shelters." He eats another ring. "She's too young to be on her own."

"I agree." This kid's barely any older.

Jaw Knee Boy licks his fingers and grins. "I love onion rings." He takes another bite of the burger.

"Do you have any idea where she was from?"

"Why'd you say *was*? Is she dead?" When I nod, he sets the burger on the bag. Green-tinged sadness tugs the corners of his eyes, then swirls across his cheeks. "Oh." He swallows. Licks his lips. "That's too bad. I liked her."

"I'm sorry you lost a friend."

Picking up the burger, he licks the ketchup oozing from the side. "I haven't seen her for a while. Guess that's why." He takes another bite.

"So ..." My husky voice falters. I need to think about taking a breath. "Did she ever say where she's from?"

He scrunches his face. "Down south somewhere. By some nuke-u-lar tanks. Said they used to sneak in and try to climb them." His eyes wander, then return to me. "In Yelma? Is that a place?"

"Elma. It's near the Satsop nuclear plant. The cooling towers were all that got built." That'll be difficult to visit without a car. "Do you know her last name, or did she mention brothers or sisters?"

"She has a older sister. Way older, like twenty. She wasn't livin' at home, but she was close by." He pushes his finger through an onion ring, lifts it to his mouth. "Did I say how much I like rings?" He gives me a crooked grin and pops it in. "Linda. Did ya know that means *pretty* in Spanish? That's her sister's name." He finishes off the rings. "Man, I'm gettin' full."

"What about a last name?"

"Hmm." Nibbling on the remains of the burger, he bites the meat even with the bun. "It was somethin' boring, y'know, like Johnson or Thompson or somethin' like that."

"That's really helpful." I sit with him as he finishes the burger and tries to drain the last drops sticking to the milkshake cup. He scrapes his finger around the inside as far as he can reach, then slurps off the chocolaty goo and shoves the cup into the bag. After licking his fingers, he wipes his hands on his jeans. I'm sad about the situation this boy finds himself in, but try to smile. "I hope you enjoyed your meal."

"I haven't been this full since the Teen Feed holiday party back at Christmas." He flops to his back and rubs his belly, then raises his head. A flash draws my eyes to his neck—a jagged chunk of obsidian hanging from a nylon cord. My stomach rumbles. I force my focus to his eyes. His aura has transitioned to a warm purplish satisfaction. "They gave me new socks and underwear."

"I appreciate everything you told me." I get to my feet.

"I wish I could do more than buy you a meal, but I'm in a bit of a bind right now."

He gets up and brushes off his pants. "I'm doin' OK." He nods. "Considerin' the state of the world." Even though I'm low on cash, I pull out a twenty and press it into his hand. His eyes grow wide. "Thanks!"

I smile. "Let me give you a number. If you need help, call this woman. Her name's Maggie." Taking his phone, I type in the number. "Tell her Rix sent you. She's really nice."

"You're pretty cool." He turns toward The Ave. "See ya 'round."

No longer in the mood for hunting, I head back to the motel. Besides, I need to work. In my room, I login. The image of Corvina lying next to my keyboard keeps drawing my eyes. I open the map app and plot a course to Elma. I've got loose ends to tie up.

July 14 to 16, 2020
Rix

I take buses down to the airport, where I found a cheap car rental place. For a minimal extra charge, they'll allow me to use a different drop-off location, in the very likely case that I don't bring the car back to SeaTac. When the agent at the counter calls for "Mr Ritchie"—my new name's Andrew Ritchie—I don't immediately respond. I can easily remember it, but still need to get used to people calling me that. What first name should I use? Maybe Andy? I've never been Andy before. Do I seem more like Andy, or Andrew? Or maybe just Drew? There was a time in my life when I answered to Andrews, my family name, so either way, an easy transition. Over the years, it's become more and more difficult and costly to procure quality forged documents, more time-consuming to open new accounts, and trickier to use the right channels to move assets around without getting tracked. I rushed it this time. If it doesn't work out, I'll pick another name and start again from scratch.

At eleven, I leave SeaTac behind. The bright urban lights continue until I'm beyond Olympia, where darkness abruptly overtakes me, as if I'm leaving one life behind and driving into the great unknown. It's nearly twelve-thirty when I don my mask and register at the Parkhurst Motel. In my room, I empty my backpack of all but my laptop. No point in risking the loss of another one. I shoulder the pack and go for a stroll. Elma's a very small town. No one else is out walking around. The only thing open is the convenience store, where I wander up and down the aisles for a few minutes before grabbing a bottle of water. It'll give me a reason to talk to the clerk.

At the cash register, she's chatty. Probably doesn't get many customers these days. "Hi, doll. New in town?"

"Just here for a couple of nights." I take out a five. As she makes change, I add, "I bet you know everyone in town."

She lays the bills and coins on the counter. "Everyone in the valley. It's hard not to."

Before scooping the money into my pocket, I pull out

the picture of Corvina and lay it down. "Do you remember her?"

"The Thompson girl. She ran away last winter."

"Do you know where I can find her family? Maybe her sister, Linda?" I hope Jaw Knee Boy's information was correct.

"Sure. She tends bar down at the Alibi Tavern, but they close at eleven." She runs her finger over the image. "Is she in trouble?"

"Something like that." I fold the paper, grab my water and head for the door. "Thanks for your help."

I spend the rest of the night and most of the day getting caught up at work. After sending in the quarterly plan, I touch base with all my team members. Nalini's being very flexible. I don't want my new ID linked to my job, so I just told her I lost my phone. The intermittent wifi slows me down, but it's all I can expect at a cheap motel in the middle of nowhere. Everyone at work is forced to use texts or email if they want to talk to me, which will make it easier until I get settled somewhere.

After the golden glow of the setting sun fades, I grab my backpack and head down Main Street to the Alibi—under new management, so now it's a sports bar, the New Alibi Station. When I enter, small clusters of patrons look me up and down. Few wear masks. I'm not in Seattle anymore. I sit at the bar. Every other stool has an X taped to it. The social distancing should keep the conversation relatively private.

When the bartender comes to take my order, she bears an uncanny resemblance to Corvina. They're definitely related. "What can I get ya, honey?" She smiles, but her voice is hard.

"Tequila?" My eyes wander to the upper shelf. "Herradura reposado. Neat."

"I like a man with class." Her smile seems more genuine, but she's probably after a bigger tip. She returns a minute later and sets down a very full shot glass of amber liquid. "Careful, hon. I overfilled it."

She goes back to her work.

As I slowly sip my drink, the bar gets more crowded, well ... in pandemic terms. If I was susceptible, I'd definitely feel uncomfortable in a room with this many unmasked people. When my glass is nearly empty, she returns from serving, sweaty and flushed. What a hard life. "How's it going, hon? You want another one?"

I wouldn't normally, but I need an excuse to linger. "Please, but first, tell me your name?"

"I'm Linda."

"You can call me ... Andy."

On the front page of an abandoned newspaper, I read about the nightly protests in Portland where things have really blown up since the feds arrived. Can I join a group of medics there? By the time my second shot's half gone, the bar has quieted. I look around. In the back, a couple huddles in the privacy of a booth. At a nearby table, three young men talk animatedly about Seattle's new NHL team, the Kraken.

"What a stupid name," one of them says.

I don't really follow sports, but I do like hockey, so I eavesdrop.

"I kinda like it."

"Can't wait for the first game, but that's not til 2021."

At the other end of the bar, Linda chats with the only other patron, an older man with tough, creased skin, like old leather, and missing teeth. When she begins wiping the bar, moving in my direction, he keeps talking, his hand rising as if the gesture could capture the moment. I know that feeling. He slips off his stool and weaves out the door.

When Linda's towel brushes my hand, she looks up and smiles. "Sorry. Ready for another one?"

I put my palm over the glass. "No, thanks." I return her smile "Two's more than my limit. Especially your pours." I reach in my pocket. "I need to talk to you."

As she hangs the towel, she watches me suspiciously, then leans on the bar. "What is it, hon?" When I open the paper, laying it with Corvina's image facing her, the color leaves her face. "What's she done?"

"Is she your sister?"

"Yeah. Is she all right?" Her flat tone and the flash of tangerine to her cheeks tell me she knows she's not.

"What time do you get off?"

"Eleven." She glances at the clock over the bar, then stands upright and hollers, "Last call."

I look over my shoulder. The couple has already disappeared. The squeak of chairs announces the departure of the hockey fans.

"G'night, Linda."

"See you tomorrow."

One blows her a kiss.

Behind them, Linda locks the front door, then turns

off the neon *open* sign. She sits at the nearest table and pats it. "Come tell me what you know."

When I sit next to her, I'm uncertain what's safe to share. "She was staying with this boy." I turn over the paper. "She got sick, with COVID, and he took her in. Well, he found them shelter. He was homeless, too."

"Why didn't she come to me?" she whispers.

"Maybe she just needed to get away."

"I couldn't protect her." Her shoulders droop in resignation. "I couldn't even protect myself." A tear drops, landing on the corner of the paper. Linda flicks it away. "Mom made some bad decisions, but Buddy's the worst of all." Another tear escapes. "When did she die?"

"A few days ago."

She steps to the bar for a napkin and daubs at her eyes. "Why'd you come? Did CPS send you?"

"I've spent some time on the streets, too. I just knew her." I restrain myself from touching Linda's hand, wishing I could provide some comfort. "I wanted you to know. I wasn't sure the cops would bother finding you."

"All right." Her voice sounds frail. "Well, thanks for coming. I appreciate the effort. I need to clean up now and get home to let the sitter go." She walks me to the door and locks it behind me.

July 17, 2020
Rix

After letting Corvina go, I slept peacefully for the first time since before the raid. It might have been due to total exhaustion from lack of sleep, but letting Linda know probably had something to do with it. Now, my mind is consumed by Erlandr. I think back on the clues he mentioned—missing Ireland and the heather—and do some research to try to find his family. He didn't have an Irish accent, so I search for *Ireland, Washington.* Sure enough, it's in the Cascade foothills east of Vancouver. I look for a heather farm and find *Ireland Organic Heather.* I start there.

Fields of purple and pink lie nestled in a pleasant little valley of woods and farmland. The sign by the road says, *Farm Closed Due to COVID*, but I turn up the long, winding drive. To either side, heather shrubs stretch into the darkness. When I reach a rustic cabin, I turn off the car and don my mask. A hand-painted sign over the screened-in porch reads *Mhamó's.* I'm certain Erlandr used that name. This must be the place. As I get out, a floodlight comes on, making me squint. Someone steps onto the dimly lit porch, silently puffing a pipe. The grind of gravel under my feet fills the night with sound. As I near, I make out a small woman with weathered brown skin and a couple of gnarled knuckles on the hand that holds the pipe.

"Good evening," I call. "Are you Mhamó?"

"Only one person calls me that, and he's gone." She peers at me through the screen door, then holds it open. "You may come in."

I'm glad I didn't need to ask. That myth *is* true. As I follow her inside, I pull the picture of Erlandr from my pocket.

"Erlandr"—she draws deeply on her weird little pipe, and gently blows the smoke down my body, beginning at my head—"is a name I haven't spoken in some time." As she walks around me, she puffs and blows, reminding me of a steam engine, then stops to study my face. "No need for that mask, is there?" After waiting for me to pocket it, she takes another small puff and blows directly at my face. "You should breathe some in." As I inhale, my shoulders relax. She studies me, then smiles faintly. "Most men would no longer be standing." On a thick, geometrically patterned rug by the waning fire, she sits with her legs crossed and pats the spot across from her. "Sit."

I glance at the door before dropping to the floor, and sit sideways, so I can keep an eye on it. It's always best to be able to see the exits.

"No no no." She pats directly in front of her. "Here, with your knees against mine."

I scoot to the designated spot, like I often sit with Maggie. *Sat*—like I so often *sat* with her. When Mhamó holds out her hands, I put mine in hers. The knuckles are no longer arthritic. Her skin is lighter and more supple. Am I seeing through a charm? Raising my gaze to her dark eyes, I'm lost. My peripheral vision tells me she's speaking—her mouth moves—but I hear nothing. It's so peaceful. I can't remember the last time I felt this much calm. I just want to stay here.

Faint words break the spell. "... his father ... my daughter, Ciara ... that bastard ... just four ... came to be with me

... renamed him Doran ... *stranger* in Gaelic ... he called me Mhamó, you can, too ... CPS deemed me unfit ... foster home after foster home ... named himself Erlandr, which also means *stranger*,"—the words grow louder—"but is much older. It suited him."

"It did." Was that me speaking? I pull my eyes away from her inky pools to watch the flickering flames behind her. "He was so quiet. Almost like he wasn't there."

"Was he?" she asks.

I blink, bringing my eyes to her face. What does she mean? "W-what?"

"Was he really there? Or was he just a ghost?"

"He was a vampire." Why'd I say that?

When she offers her pipe, I shake my head. She draws on it. "You are, too—a ghost caught between two realms." I nod. She disappears behind the smoke for a moment. "He's safe now." In the remains of the fire, a smoldering log loudly pops, causing an eruption of dancing red embers. My eyes try to follow each one as they shoot up the flue. "Do you have a safe place?" Her words draw my focus to her.

"I thought I did." I shake my head. "I lost her."

She drops my hands and pats my knee. "You'll find her again, my dear."

End of Volume Four: Vampire Roundup

ACKNOWLEDGMENTS

My heartfelt thanks goes out to all my people who encouraged and supported me while writing this work.

My mother, Mary, for her never-ending support of this endeavor.

My editor, Coral Alejandra Moore (https://www.coralmoore.com/).

My cover artist, Jamie Noble Frier (https://thenobleartist.com/).

My entire writing community, including all the folks who've listened to me read and given me encouragement at Two Hour Transport and 2am Notes. Special shoutout to Seelye, Keyan, Nicole and Ellen, who read all four volumes that make up books one and two and who gave me invaluable feedback.

My niece, Pam, for insider info on the state of her ER during the pandemic.

Nisi Shawl and K Tempest Bradford of Writing The Other (https://writingtheother.com/) and Cascade Writer's Group (http://cascadewriters.com/) for scholarships to attend workshops when I was unable to afford them. DreamFoundry (https://dreamfoundry.org/) for letting me attend workshops.

What the Fuck Just Happened Today (https://whatthe

fuckjusthappenedtoday.com/) for copious notes on political events. Donations are accepted here: https://whatthefuckjusthappenedtoday.com/membership/.

Wikipedia (https://en.wikipedia.org/wiki/Main_Page) and its contributors for numerous citations. You can donate to them here: https://wikimediafoundation.org/support/.

AUTHOR'S NOTE

Rix is a manifestation of my anxiety triggered by the Sars-CoV-2 (COVID-19) pandemic in the opening months of 2020. Like many, many other creative folks, I found I could not focus on my current work. I was writing another vampire series of novels, and preparing a backstory novel for publication. I just couldn't. I did feel compelled to write, though, unlike so many of my writer friends. All I could manage were dystopian flash fiction pieces related to the pandemic. They depressed even me. Then one day, as they are wont to do, a vampire walked into a story. One flash became three. Expanding them into a short story became a rudimentary novella. Then I couldn't stop. Rix became the vehicle for me to document the events I was witnessing. And those didn't stop either. So one novella became a novel in two volumes, and then a second novel emerged to set the stage for a potential series of eight or more novels.

I had never written before in first person, present

tense but all my pandemic writings came out this way. Rix relates what I observed: the empty store shelves; the violent summer of 2020 (for me, live-streamed on the platform formerly known as Twitter); huge communities of unhoused folks; boarded up windows on businesses; empty freeways; protester abductions; migrant detentions. But I'm getting ahead of myself.

I included the Footnotes section after Volume Four in the ebook edition to help readers remember the specifics of the times this story documents, and to have access to content warnings, if they want to explore them before reading the story. The Footnotes are available on my website at https://www.ramonaridgewell.com/footnotes-strength-of-a-vampire, for those print book readers, and anyone else, who are interested in following up with events cited in this work. It felt important to me to be accurate in my retelling of these times. We need to remember.

PUBLICATION HISTORY

"**Vampires Walk at Night**," a short collection of scifaiku included in "Eccentric Orbits: An Anthology Of Science Fiction Poetry Volume 4," DimensionFold (2023).

"**Vampire Seasons**," a short collection of scifaiku included in "Eccentric Orbits: An Anthology Of Science Fiction Poetry Volume 4," DimensionFold (2023).

"**Wildfires**," a short collection of scifaiku included in "Eccentric Orbits: An Anthology Of Science Fiction Poetry Volume 5," DimensionFold (2024).

"**Containment**," a speculative poem included in "Eccentric Orbits: An Anthology Of Science Fiction Poetry Volume 5," DimensionFold (2024).

An excerpt from the novel, "**Being a Vampire: Seattle Vampire Tales Book One**," included in "Two Hour Transport Anthology 2," Fairwood Press (2024).

"**Being a Vampire: Seattle Vampire Tales Book One**," Intrepid Turtle Press (2024).

"**Strength of a Vampire - Seattle Vampire Tales Book Two**," Intrepid Turtle Press (2025)

Co-editor, with NIB and Keyan Bowes, of "**Two Hour Transport Anthology 2**," Fairwood Press (2024).

UPCOMING BOOKS

"**Blood of a Vampire**" continues Rix's story. Things get much darker as he learns the truth about where vampires end up when they are abducted. Coming April 2025 from Intrepid Turtle Press.

Find it here: https://www.ramonaridgewell.com/svt-b3-blood-of-a-vampire

Here's a couple of paragraphs from the first scene:

As I slowly walk down the street, I check the map app on my phone to see which direction to go. A black van screeches to a halt ahead of me. Half a dozen black-clad soldiers stream out. I look around and see no one else. I'm a clearly marked medic. Why do they want me? Oh. Oh, no! Locking my phone, I toss it into the bushes. These men look just like the ones who abducted David and Azul. They surround me, jerking my arms behind me, binding my hands—too tight—with a zip tie. It cuts into my wrists. They drag me into the van and shove me onto a bench seat along the side.

A flashlight blinds me. My mask is ripped away. "Hold him tight." Moving closer, the one in charge presses his fingers to my neck. "Be careful." His triumphant smile is haloed in canary self-assurance. "This one's special." He slides a rough black bag over my head. "Let's get outta here."

ABOUT THE AUTHOR

Besides writing dystopian flash fiction and epic vampire novels, Ramona Ridgewell (she/her) has had two poems published in the speculative poetry anthology, "Eccentric Orbits Volume 4: An Anthology Of Science Fiction Poetry (2023)," and two poems in "Eccentric Orbits 5: An Anthology of Science Fiction Poetry (2024)." She co-edited "Two Hour Transport Anthology: 2 (2024)," which contains an excerpt from this, her debut novel, "Being a Vampire: Seattle Vampire Tales Book One (2024)." Her days are spent tapping on a keyboard to create pretty software. She also seeks out adventures, near and far; lures melodies from her piano, guitar and vocal cords; and experiments with combinations of edible ingredients—recipes are just guidelines. Although no little furries currently share her home, crows from the neighborhood murder follow her on her walks and drop little gifts to gain her affection. A proud member of the Dreamcrashers, she thrives in the Two Hour Transport community where she is part of the management team.

She can be found at www.ramonaridgewell.com, or on Instagram @ramonaridgewellwrites.